# Book 1

# THE SECRET LIFE OF TRUMP

"""

Adapted by
**Xnonymous Y NIMUS**

Disclaimer: This is a work of Fiction. Names, Characters, Businesses, places, events and incidents are used in a fictitious manner.

ISBN: 978-0-9921724-1-1

# Table of Contents

Introduction

## Chapter 1 X Childhood and parents

## Chapter 2 X Trump's school

# Chapter 3 X Trump's Career

## Chapter 4 X Melanie's school days

## Chapter 5 X Melanie's career

## Chapter 6 X Melanie's dating background

## Chapter 7 X Trump's married life

## Chapter 8 X Cheating in the couple's lives

## Chapter 9 X Trump is overwhelmed and goes crazy

## Chapter 10 X Old Age, Death and after the death of Trump

## Chapter 11 X Conclusion

# Acknowledgements

XY Nimus, the author, would like to thank all those who have made the publication of this book possible.

A Big Thanks to the great American people for voting him into office and providing the world with such an inspiration.

**Follow the author on Twitter @nimus_y (NimusUnderscoreY) to get updates on new releases and also new exciting merchandise coming out soon**

## <u>Dedication:</u>

This book is dedicated to the most controversial man in his time. Hated and loved by many, one thing is sure; he is not a hypocrite and always speaks his mind. Controversial is who he likes to be. He probably means well but his ways are not always unanimous. He chooses what he believes to be right and sticks with it.

# Introduction

This book is a combination of jokes that have been collected, adapted and given life through a character named Trump. The reason is to bring some light, laughter and joy to the lives of those who read it.

The main character of the book is a fictional character who lived somewhere near North West Asia.

The book tells the story of a very strange and unique man whose life has been full of interesting and humorous stories. The man's main ancestors were from Africa; His father was from Russia and his mother from India. He was born in Europe, grew up in Asia, and married a woman from the Arctic. He worked in all five continents and his place of death is still unknown.

After his autobiography was discovered, archaeologists set their minds to locate his remains, to analyze them and to try to understand this unique and interesting person. They are still searching and once they discover his remains, maybe we will be able to resurrect him and see if he can bring some joy to this globally depressed world.

The book follows Trump from his birth to his death. It deals with his childhood, his career, and other interesting episodes in his life. It also includes a background on Trump's most prominent and influential wife, the one with whom he shared the most important part of his life and the one that knew him and understood him the most.

In case you don't understand some parts of the book or you are lost in the logic of the book; don't worry, just take it one joke at a time.

# Chapter 1x Childhood and parents

*Trump was born into a middle class family. Early on in his life, he showed signs of being a troubled kid. Maybe it was due to his complicated and contradictory origins and upbringing.*

## 1. The train is late

Little Trump was only two years old when he was playing with his train next to his mom while she was ironing clothes. Little Trump said "tchoo tchoo, arrival at Rockbay Station, station of crooks," his mom warned him against his language. Trump continued his tour, "tchoo tchoo, Station of Manha, station of the retarded," his mom told him to go to his room and that he was grounded for two hours. Later Trump's mom let him out of his room and allowed him to continue playing. Trump continued his tour "tchoo tchoo, Station of Brooks, two hours late due to a bitch"

*Trump's mom worried so much about his bad behavior and strong language, that she embarked on a radical new way to educate him and concentrated most of her efforts on eliminating obscene words from Trump's vocabulary and she even took it to a new level.*

## 2. A worried mother

Little Trump's mother is so worried about his manners that she gave him some guidance on appropriate things to say in front of people. "From now on, when you need to go to the toilet, instead of saying, mom I want to go to the toilet, you will say, Mom, I want to sing." His mom instructed. Trump followed her advice. The next weekend, he went to stay at his Grandparents. In the middle of the night, he called his Grandma. "Grandma, I want to sing!"

"Not now," said Grandma, "you will have time to do that tomorrow, now please let me sleep."

"But Trump kept insisting, until Grandma gave in."

"Alright, but don't wake your Grandfather! Do it quietly in my ear ...."

*A change in Trump's vocabulary did not help to change his ways. He was still a very naughty boy and from time to time, he got some of his siblings into his troubles as well.*

## 3. Revenge Gone Bad

Trump was a very naughty boy and was always involved in fights. One day he met a boy named Pence who beat him up, like he had never been beaten before. So he decided to recruit his brother to avenge him. His brother, being an idiot, immediately attacked Pence. Pence beat up Trump's brother as well and he was beaten up more severely than Trump. When Trump and his brother were on their way home, both badly beaten, Trump's brother, with tears in his eyes, started beating up Trump.

hhhm, hjds, slap, ... "Trump why didn't you tell me that the boy was so strong. If I knew I would not have got involved, look what he has done to me."

*Subsequently Trump befriended Pence and they became best friends.*
*Trump arrived home to find his father drinking Vodka as only a typical Russian knew how. His father usually drank all day.*

## 4. Vodka Love

Trump's father was sitting at his usual place in the kitchen, drinking his vodka.

Trump walked in and said,

"Dad, the price of vodka has increased; does that mean you will drink less?"

"No son, it means you will eat less."

*Even though Trump was a desperate case, his mother always defended him and blamed others for his mistakes. Today the guilty one was his best friend Pence who was being blamed for being a bad influence on Trump.*

## 5. An Angry Mother

Trump's mother was particularly angry with Pence today.
"Trump! I forbid you from going to Pence's house because he has very bad manners. But little Trump really wanted to play with his friend."
"Mom, because I am so well behaved, can Pence come over here?"

*Trump was off to bed and he was very thirsty*

## 6. Thirsty in bed

Little Trump got settled into his bed, five minutes later he called, "Daaaaaaaaaaaaaaaaaad!"
"WHAT?"
"I am thirsty; can you bring me a glass of water?" "No, go to sleep."
Five minutes later.
"Daaaaaaaaaaaaaaaaaaaaaaaaaaaaad!"
"WHAT?"
"I am thirsty; please can you bring me a glass of water?"
"I said no, if you ask me again, I am going to get up, to punish you." Five minutes later.
"Daaaaaaaaaaaaaaaaaaaad!"
"WHAT?"
"When you get up to punish me, can you also bring me a glass of water?"

*The next day, Trump was hanging out with Pence.*
*Trump's neighbor was getting married, so they*
*both sat outside and watched the guests arrive and*
*saw the ceremony take place. After the ceremony,*
*Trump remarked to Pence that he noticed*
*something odd.*

## 7. The Bride changed her mind

After the ceremony, Trump said to his friend Pence:
"Did you see what happened?"
"What?"
"The bride changed her mind in the church"

"What makes you say that, Trump?"

"Because, I saw her going down the aisle in the arms of an old man

and came out in the arms of a young man.

*After the wedding, after all the guests had left, Trump found a woman's handbag lying around, so he decided to return the handbag to its owner. Even though Trump was a very naughty boy, he was very honest.*

## 8. Give me a reward and I don't want to hear excuses

A woman lost her handbag in the crowd of a wedding; luckily Trump who is a very honest kid, rushed around to find the lady. When he found her, the woman was very happy to be reunited with her bag and delighted to discover that there were still honest kids out there.

She opened her bag, nothing was missing. However, something surprised her. She asked Trump:

"It's weird, when I lost my handbag, there was a twenty dollar note inside but now there are four five dollar notes."

"Yes ma'am, the last time I returned a woman's bag that had

a twenty dollar note inside, the woman did not reward me,

she pretended that she did not have any change.

*Trump got his five dollars and went home. He was in his room, unusually quiet; which made his mother worried.*

## 9. Help me finish this 'nothing' I am doing

Trump's mom asked him,

"What are you doing Trump?"

"Nothing!"

"What about your brother?"

"He is helping me!"

*Little Trump was a very curious boy and decided to accompany his father to the opera. He was amazed and puzzled by what he witnessed.*

## 10. At the opera

"Dad, who is the man scaring that lady with his big gestures?" "He is not scaring her; he is the conductor of the orchestra." "So why is the woman screaming?"

*Trump returned home from the opera and he went straight to see his mom, as he was missing her and wanted to clarify some things that he had heard that day.*

## 11. Family origins

"Mom, Dad says that we all come from monkeys in Africa, is that true?" "I have no idea; your father has always refused to talk about his family."

*Trump's mom was having her hair made, Trump sat there quietly and observed.*

## 12. Why do you have Grey Hair?

He was sitting next to her while she was having her hair washed. All of a sudden, he noticed that his mother had some gray hair. "Mom, why are some of your hairs grey?"
"Well, every time you do something bad and make me cry or hurt my feelings, one of my hairs turns grey."
"Ok, Now I understand why all Grandmas' hairs are grey."

# Chapter 2 x Trump's school

As you might expect, Trump graduated from primary school but quit Secondary school because he couldn't wait to start making money. Trump found first and second grade boring. He was taught that graduating from school was the guaranteed way to success but when he observed his father, who had various degrees and a PhD, lose jobs and struggle to make a living, it made him realize that this was what the real world was about. Trump began to lose the focus and the motivation to study.

*Little Trump had just changed schools when he went to third grade and he was disappointed with his new teacher.*

## 13. The teacher is harassing me, I want out

After the first day he told his mother that he didn't want to go back to that school anymore, even though he had just joined the school. His mother asked him why?

"Well, he replied, the teachers in that school are all so ignorant.

They are always asking questions!"

*Today was the second day of grade three and they now had a new teacher, who used to practice as a psychologist.*

## 14. The new teacher was a psychologist

The new teacher in Trump's class was a psychologist before joining the school.

She stood up and said,

"All those who have felt a little bit stupid today, stand up!" No one stood up, but after a few minutes, Trump stood up. The teacher said,

"So you have felt a bit stupid today?"

"No, but I felt bad letting you be the only one standing."

## 15. Unusual behavior

The class assignment was to write about something unusual that had happened during the past week. The next day little Trump got up to read his homework. "Dad fell in the stairs last week." He began. "Good heavens" said the teacher. "Is he all right now?" "He must be" said little Trump. "He stopped yelling for help yesterday."

*Later that day, the teacher asked for a volunteer to say a full sentence.*

## 16. Switch off the light let me eat that thing

Little Trump was sitting in class with his fellow peers. The teacher asked for a volunteer to say a sentence. When no one raised their hand, the teacher called on Little Trump to say the full sentence. He replied with "Hummm... Well... My brother eats light bulbs." The teacher looked at Trump strangely and said "Oh no, Trump, your brother doesn't eat light bulbs, that's absurd"
Trump argued back "Yes, last night my brother said to his wife

'oh honey, turn off that lamp and let me eat that thing."

*Now it's time for the science class and a little experience to educate the young minds*

## 17. Why is that worm sinking in the liquor?

Little Trump was in science class. The teacher was conducting an experiment to show the dangers of liquor. He had one glass of water and one glass of wine. So the professor started the experiment and he stuck one worm in the water. It floated around and looked happy. He stuck the other worm in the wine and it looked like it was struggling to breathe and then it sunk to the bottom and died. So the teacher asked, "What is this suppose to teach you children?" No one raised their hand to answer but then after a while little Trump raised his hand and said "drink liquor and you won't get worms."

*Because of his misinterpretation of the experiment, the teacher punished Trump by asking him to write an essay on worms, so he decided to do some research at the library. An unfortunate thing happened to him there.*

## 18. Come open the library so I can go home

Trump was phoning the librarian

"What time does the library open?" he asked.

"9 a.m." came the reply. "Why are you calling me in the middle of the night to ask a question like that?" the librarian asked.

"Not until 9 a.m.?" Trump sighed in a disappointed tone.

"Yes that is correct, we do not open until nine in the morning," the librarian said. "Why are you so desperate to get into the library?" "Who said I wanted to get in?" Trump said sadly. "I want to get out."

*Trump finally got out of the library. He had been so traumatized about being locked in there, that he went to the teacher to inform her that he was unable to do his homework.*

## 19. Why would you punish me? I didn't do it.

At school Trump raced into the corridor, shouting,

"Teacher!!!!! Teacher!!!!!!!!!!!!"

"Yes Trump?"

"Can you punish someone for something he didn't do?"

"Of course not, why?"

"Because I didn't do my homework!!!"

*Trump got another chance to do his homework and the teacher informed him that this time he would be punished if he didn't do his homework.*

## 20. Don't mess with me when I am drunk

The teacher gave her fifth grade class an assignment.

The assignment was to ask their parents to tell them a story with a moral at the end of it.

The next day, the kids came back and one by one began to tell their stories.

"Trump, do you have a story to share?" asked the teacher

"Yes, ma'am, my Daddy told a story about my Aunty. My Aunty was a pilot in Desert Storm and her plane got hit. She had to bail out over enemy territory and all she had was a small flask of whiskey, a pistol and a survival knife. She drank the whiskey on the way down so it wouldn't fall into enemy hands and then her parachute landed right in the middle of twenty enemy troops. She shot fifteen of them with the gun until she ran out of bullets, killed four more with the knife, until the blade broke and then she killed the last one with her bare hands."

"Good heavens" said the horrified teacher, "What kind of moral did your daddy teach you from that horrible story?"

"Stay the hell away from Aunty when she's been drinking."

*After hearing this drinking story, the teacher decided to invite President G.W. Bush, who had recovered from a drinking problem, to tell the class about his experiences with his drinking problem and to motivate the class to take their school work seriously.*

## 21. G.W. Bush is teaching kids about war

G.W. Bush went to the primary school to talk about the war and other issues. After his talk he asked if anyone had any questions. Little Pence puts up his hand and Bush asks him what his name is. "Pence" he responded. "And your question is, Pence?" "I have three questions to ask Sir; firstly, why did the USA invade Iraq without the support of the UN? Secondly, why are you President when Al Gore got more votes? And thirdly, whatever happened to Osama Bin Laden?" Just then the bell rang for break. G.W. Bush informed the children that they would continue after recess.

When they resumed, Bush said, "OK, where were we? Oh that's right question time. Who has a question?" Little Trump puts up his hand, Bush points him out and asks him what his name is. "Trump" "And what is your question, Trump?" "I have five questions for you Sir. First, why did the USA invade Iraq without the support of the UN? Second, why are you President when Al Gore got more votes? Third, whatever happened to Osama Bin Laden? Fourth, why did the recess bell go off twenty minutes early? And fifth, what the fuck happened to Pence?"

## 22. Allow me to introduce my....

During the class on good manners, the teacher asked her students, "If you were having dinner with a girl from a good family and had to go to the bathroom to relieve yourself, how would you tell her?"

One student replied, "Wait here for a second; I'm going to take a pee."

"That would be bad manners and inappropriate, how would you say it Pence?" responded the teacher

"Excuse me, I need to go to the toilet, but I'll back" he replied.

"That's slightly better, but it's unpleasant to mention toilets while eating. How about you Trump, would you be able to say it, in a better way?"

"I would say, baby, I would like to apologize to leave you for a moment, I am going to give a hand to a very intimate friend of mine that I am hoping to introduce you to after dinner."

*At the end of the day, Trump and his friends were on their way home. They were discussing their parents.*

## 23. My father works for the government

"My father is the fastest man on earth! He drives an ambulance. He leaves the hospital at two o clock and within eight minutes, he is home." said the first one

"My father is the fastest man on earth! He flies a Concord. He leaves Montréal at two o clock and two hours later he is in New York." said the second one

"My father is the fastest, he works for the government! He works until five and at half past three, he is at home." said Trump

*Still on their way home, talking about whose father was faster, they saw a pole protruding from the pavement.*
*Trump and Pence were standing at the base of a flagpole, looking up, in an effort to guess the height of the pole.*

## 24. We want to know the height, not the length

A woman walked by and asked what they were doing. "We're supposed to find the height of the flagpole," said Pence, "but we don't have a ladder."

The woman took a wrench from her purse, loosened a few bolts, and laid the pole down. Then she took a tape measure from her pocket, took a measurement and announced, "5 feet" and walked away. Trump shook his head and laughed. "Isn't that just like a dumb woman? We ask for the height, and she gives us the length!"

*They carried on walking after the pole incident.*
*They noticed a blind man standing at a traffic light,*
*on a cross road, for quite some time.*

## 25. Blind man's Guide dog

The man had his guide-dog next to him. The traffic light changed to green and the dog didn't move. Then it changed to red. Moments later, the traffic light changed to green again and the dog still didn't move. Then the traffic light changed to red again. This went on for a while and Trump decided to do something about it.

He walked up to the blind man and asked,

"Hey, wasn't your dog supposed to help you cross the road when the traffic light turned green?"

"Yes; why?"

"Because the traffic light turned green many times and your dog didn't move"

"Thank you for telling me" said the blind man

Then the blind mind searched in his pocket and took out a lump of sugar that he gave to the dog and the dog immediately ate it.

Trump was confused and said to the blind man:

"Your dog is not doing his job and you are rewarding him for it?" The blind man replied:

"No, that was only to find where his head is! Now he is going to get a sharp kick up the backside."

*Pence was telling Trump about this new IM application (instant Messaging). He told him about all the new girls that he was meeting there. Pence signed him up as well and now Trump had an account on the app.*

## 26. Who are you really chatting with, somebody's Grandma?

Little Trump was on Messenger SIO (secret is out) pretending to be older than he is. He was chatting to on old lady who was also pretending to be younger and he got her number. He started calling her and they spoke for hours about all kinds of stuff. He even told the woman, he was going to marry her.

They had a date at the lady's house and the lady invited all the members of her family. Her house was crowded with family members.

Trump was on his way to her. He decided to phone her, to make sure that he was in the correct neighborhood.

"Hello, I am here by the Jobless Head Quarters, which way should I go?'

"Turn to your right after the station and it's the first house on the left" she said.

"Okay, I am by your door, are you coming outside or should I come in?"

"Come in," she said.

Trump walked in to see a house packed full of people waiting for him. They all had their eyes fixed on him. He was so shocked and scared that he immediately fainted.

He was woken up and he realized what situation he was in, He started crying, "I was juuust playinnng arouuund, I aammm sorry...." he said.

The woman told him not to cry and that they were just going to have the wedding ceremony and it would all be over.

He cried even louder, "Please don't do that to me, I am just a little kid, I promise I will never do it again."

After a long plea, they decided to let him go and from then on, Trump decided that he will only use Twitter and not chat with anyone.

*The moral of the story is that people on the net are not always What they pretend to be. You could probably be chatting to someone younger than your children or older than your Grandma.*
*The next day three students were summoned to the principal's office for behaving badly during school hours.*

## 27. Paper is thrown out the window

The principal was interrogating them.

"You, Pen, what have you done?"

"I have sprayed graffiti on the classroom wall."

"Go clean that rubbish off, straight away and you will have detention on Saturday afternoon."

"What about you Pence, what have you done?" "I put three cockroaches on the teacher's chair."

"Go apologize to the teacher immediately and you will be on detention for the next two Saturdays."

"What about you, Trump, what have you done?" "I threw Paper through the window."

"Well, that is not serious compared to what your friends have done, you will not be punished."

"Get out of my office and I don't want to see you back here again." The three students left the office and a fourth student came into the office covered in bandages.

"What is your name?"

"My name is Paper, sir"

*Again Trump misbehaved and was expelled from school.*

## 28. What is wrong with that principal?

"Mom", said little Trump, I have been expelled from school for three days."

"But why?" she asked.

"Because I threw paper out of the window and the student sitting in front of me was smoking."

"That is unfair on behalf of your principal" exclaimed his mother "to expel you only for that." After all you are not responsible for your friend's behavior."

"Well, the truth is, Paper is another student and the student in

front of me was smoking because I lit his shirt on fire."

*Trump was eventually allowed to return to school after being expelled. He was very confused about all the new concepts, his teacher had introduced, that he had never heard of before. First his teacher tested his conjugating knowledge.*

## 29. Faster, faster

Trump's teacher asked him to conjugate the verb "to walk" in the present.

"I wal...k, you wal...k, he wal...ks" said Trump.

"Faster Trump, faster!" said the teacher.

"We run, you run, they run," Trump completed.

*At break time, Trump finally had a chance to talk to his best friend Pence and they talked about things that only they understood.*

## 30. Moonlight

"Do you think there are people on the moon?" said Pence.

Trump replied "Of course, because the lights are always on up there."

*Back in the classroom, Trump learned about two subjects, politics and negative numbers. He was confused and when he returned home from school he went to his father and asked him to explain negative numbers to him as he did not understand this concept.*

## 31. Negative Numbers Explained

Trump's father explained

"Well listen Trump; imagine four people got into a bus. If at the next stop, eight people got off, then four people would have to get in for the bus to be empty."

*Trump was even more confused about negative numbers and decided to ask his father about politics instead.*

## 32. Politics explained to kids

Little Trump asks his father about politics: "Dad, I need your help. Will you tell me about politics, I have homework on politics that I need to submit tomorrow and I really need your help."

After a minute of silence, his father replied:

"Well, I think the best way to explain politics to you is to make an analogy with our family. I am the capitalist and I am providing for the family. Your mother is the government because she controls

14

everything, the maid is the working class as she is working for us, and you are the people and your brother is the future generation." "I hope that will help you, with your homework."

"Thanks Dad, said Trump. I didn't really understand all that, but I will give it some thought."

That night Trump was woken by the cries of his little brother and noticed that he needed to be changed.

He went into his mom's room and tried unsuccessfully to wake her. He noticed that his father was not in the bed. He started to look for his father and found him in bed with the maid and then he decided to go back to bed.

The next morning at breakfast he told his father that last night he had finally figured out what politics was.

"Excellent" said his father "so tell me what you figured out?"

"I figured out that capitalism is fucking the working class, while the government is lying around ignoring the people and leaving future generations in shit."

*The next day, the teacher is amazed that Trump actually did his homework and got all the answers right, she doesn't believe it*

## 33. Who did it?

When Trump was at school:

"Trump, confess that your father helped you to do your homework" said the teacher.

"No Sir, I swear! He didn't."

"Are you sure?"

"Yes, I am sure. He did it alone"

*The teacher gave the students a test, to test their knowledge on the various subjects covered, during the past week. There was a section in the test that required yes or no answers. Trump had a technique he used for these types of questions.*

## 34. Yes or No? Toss the coin, time is running out

The teacher asked his students a series of questions that required a yes or no answer; Trump started repeatedly flipping a coin in the air. This caught the teacher's attention.

"What are you doing?" asked the teacher.

"I am finding out answers by tossing this coin" replied
Trump. "Tales is yes and heads is no."
The time was up and the teacher was collecting the exam papers,
the teacher noticed that Trump was still tossing the coin but now at
a faster pace.
"What are you still doing Trump?" asked the teacher.
"I am quickly checking my answers sir!"

*After school, Trump realized that the test was*
*catastrophic for him and he prayed for a miracle.*

## 35. London the capital of Italy?

"Oh look dad, a falling star!" exclaimed Trump.
"I hope you had time to make a wish" said his dad.
"Yes, I hope it will come true, otherwise tomorrow I will get a
zero for geography!"
"Is that so? What was your wish?"
"That London became the capital of Italy, before the teacher

marked my test."

*Trump was not feeling well, probably due to getting zero*
*for this geography test. He went to the Doctor to see*
*what was wrong.*

## 36. Urine Analysis

Trump got to the doctor and saw a girl crying in the waiting room.
He asked her:
"Why are you crying?"
She replied:
"Because I am here for a blood
analysis" "Is that why you are crying?"
"Yes, my brother told me that they will cut one of my fingers off
to make the analysis!"
So Trump started crying too. The girl asked:
"Why are you crying now?"
"Because I am here for a urine analysis."

*His brother calmed him down and explained how the*
*test was actually done. while in the waiting room*
*Trump needs a scratch*

## 37. Remove it so you can scratch freely

At the hospital Trump was wearing a cap; he put his hand inside the cap while trying to scratch his head. Looking very ridiculous, his brother slapped him over the head and said "look at you; why can't you take your cap off to scratch your head?" Crying, Trump replied: "When you... scratch your behind, do you remove your pants?"

# Chapter 3 x Trump's Career

Trump was always street wise and a hustler. He dropped out of school, to look for a job and went to many interviews. When he went for his first interview, he had to wear the only smart clothes that he had, after the clothes cleaned was a challenge.

*And from experience, this was his advice for those who were going to an interview.*

### 38. Give me back the shirt I donated

Don't spend $2 to dry-clean a shirt. Donate it to the Salvation Army instead. They'll clean it and put it on a hanger. Next morning buy it back for seventy five cents.

*Trump's interview was in another city, so he had to take a plane to get there.*

### 39. Know shit before you talk shit

Trump was seated next to a stranger on the plane, he turned to the stranger and said, "Let's talk; I've heard that flights will go quicker if you strike up a conversation with your fellow passenger."
The stranger, who had just opened his book, closed it slowly, and said to Trump "What would you like to discuss?"
"Oh, I don't know, how about nuclear power?" said Trump
"OK" said the stranger. "That could be an interesting topic. But let me ask you a question first. "A horse, a cow, and a deer all eat grass. Yet the deer excretes little pellets, while a cow turns out a flat patty, and a horse produces clumps of dried grass. Why do you suppose that is?"

"Jeez" said Trump. "I have no idea."

"Well then" said the stranger, "How is it that you feel qualified

to discuss nuclear power when you don't know shit?"

*Trump decided to change his seat after being humiliated by the stranger, he went to look for another person to talk to and this is when he met the parrot named Twitter for the first time.*

## 40. Crash landing? Where is the plane

When he changed seats, Trump was surprised to see a parrot strapped in next to him. He asked the stewardess for coffee, just then the parrot squawked "and get me a whisky you cow!" The stewardess, flustered, brought back a whisky for the parrot and forgot the coffee. When Trump reminded her that she forgot his coffee, the parrot drained its glass and bawled "and get me another whisky you idiot." Quite upset, the girl came back shaking with another whisky but still no coffee.

Unaccustomed to such incompetence Trump decided to try the parrot's approach.

"I've asked you twice for a coffee, go and get it now, or I will make you regret being a stewardess" said Trump to the stewardess.

The next moment, both he and the parrot were wrenched up and thrown out of the emergency exit by two burly stewards.

Plunging downwards the parrot turned to him and said "For someone who can't fly, you sure do complain a lot!"

*Fortunately he survived and got to his interview on time, but he had a small problem that was jeopardizing his chances of getting the job.*

## 41. Do you want an aspirin or a condom?

Trump had a winking problem and he was applying for a position as a sales representative for a large firm. The interviewer looked over his papers and said, "This is phenomenal, you have graduated from the best primary school, your recommendations (which were fake by the way) are wonderful, and your experience is unparalleled. Normally, we would hire you without a second thought. However, a sales representative is a highly visible position, and we're afraid that

your constant winking will scare off potential customers. I'm sorry....
We can not hire you."
"But wait" he said "If I take two aspirin, I'll stop winking!"
"Really? Show me!"
So Trump reached into his jacket pocket and began pulling out all
sorts of condoms. Red condoms, blue condoms, ribbed condoms,
flavored condoms. Finally, at the bottom, he found a packet of
aspirin. He tore it open, swallowed the pills, and stopped winking.
"Well" said the interviewer "that's all well and good, but this
is a respectable company, and we will not have our
employees womanizing all over the country!"
"Womanizing? What do you mean? I'm a happily married
man!" "Well then, how do you explain all these condoms?"
"Oh, that" he sighed. "Have you ever walked into a

pharmacy, winking, and asked for aspirin?"

*Now they were about to wrap up the interview but there was
one last question for Trump.*

## 42. Why don't you pay me what I deserve?
Reaching the end of a job interview, the Human Resources
manager asked Trump "what starting salary were you looking for?"
Trump replied, "In the neighborhood of $1,250,000 a year,
depending on the benefits package."
The interviewer said "Well, what would you say to a package of
five weeks holiday, fully paid by the company, full medical and
dental cover, a company retirement fund for 50% of your salary,
and a company car leased every two years, say a black Maybach?"
Trump sat up straight and said, "Wow! Are you kidding?"
The interviewer replied, "Yes, but you started it."

*They decided to give him a chance and only a week into the
position, he almost lost his job.*

## 43. Do you know who you are talking to?
Trump was now the employee of a big firm; he picked up the
phone and randomly dialed a number and said:
"Hello baby! Shake your pretty little ass and bring me a coffee
and some cupcakes, and move it now"

On the other side of the phone a very masculine voice replied "You stupid idiot, you have the wrong number and do you know who you are talking to? I am the CEO, you idiot."

Trump then replied, "And you, sucker, do you know who you are talking to?"

"No" replied the CEO.

"Phew, thank goodness" said Trump. Relived, he hung up the phone.

**The company noticed that some of the employees were wasting a lot of time and being dishonest with the company and the client's time. So they decided to send them a memo to warn them about this.**

## 44. Memo from accounting department

*Dear Employees*

*It has come to our attention recently that many of you have been turning in time sheets that specify large amounts of "Miscellaneous Unproductive Time" which is, by the way code 3309. However, we need to know exactly what you are doing during your unproductive time.*

*Attached below is a sheet specifying a tentative extended job code list based on our observations of employee activities.*

*The list will allow you to specify with a fair amount of precision what you are doing during your unproductive time. Please begin using this job-code list immediately and let us know about any difficulties you may encounter.*

*Thanking you,*

*Accounting*

### Attached: Extended Job-Code
### List Code Description

*3310 Useless meeting.*

*3311 Trying to sound knowledgeable while in meeting.*

*3312 Waiting for break, lunch or end of the day.*

*3313 Waiting for lunch.*

*3314 Waiting for the end of day.*

*3315 Covering for incompetence of coworker friend.*

*3316 Trying to explain concept to coworker who is stupid.*

*3317 Trying to explain concept to coworker who hates you.*

*3318 Buying snack or eating snacks.*

*3319 Waiting for something to happen.*

*3320 Scratching yourself.*

*3320 Sleeping.*

*3321 Feeling bored.*

*3322 Feeling horny.*

*3323 Complaining about lousy job, low pay, long hours, coworker or the boss.*

*3324 Miscellaneous unproductive complaining.*

*3325 Not actually present at job.*

*3326 Suffering from eight-hour flu.*

*3327 Using company phone to make long distance personal calls to sell stolen company goods.*

*3328 Hiding from boss.*

*3329 Gossip.*

*3330 Feeling sorry for yourself.*

*3331 Faxing resume to another employer/headhunter.*

*3332 Pretending to work while boss is watching.*

*3333 Complaining.*

*3334 Extended visit to the bathroom. (at least 10 minutes)*

*3335 Talking with divorce lawyer on phone.*

*3336 Talking with miscellaneous paid professional on phone.*

*3337 Talking with mistress/toy boy on phone.*

*3338 Asking coworker to aid you in an illicit activity.*

*3339 Laughing while reading e-mail.*

**On his way to his lunch break, Trump got into the elevator with a lady.**

## 45. Is it T.G.I.F or S.H.I.T?

When he entered the elevator there was a blonde already inside and she greeted him by saying, "T-G-I-F".

He smiled at her and replied, "S-H-I-T."

She looked at him, puzzled, and said, "T-G-I-F" again.

He acknowledged her remark again by answering "S-H-I-T."

The blond was trying to be friendly, so she smiled her biggest smile and said as sweetly as possible "T-G-I-F" another time.

Trump smiled back to her and once again replied with a quizzical expression "S-H-I-T."

The blond finally decided to explain things, and this time she said,

"T-G-I-F, Thank Goodness it's Friday, get it?"
Trump answered "S-H-I-T, Sorry, Honey, it's Thursday".

*An incident made Trump resign from his position as he felt he received little recognition and appreciation at his current company.*

## 46. Worker dead at desk for five days

The boss at Trump's firm were trying to work out why no one noticed, that one of their employees had been seated but dead, at his desk and it took five days before anyone noticed. George, who was fifty one years old, had been employed at the company for thirty years. He had a heart attack in the open-plan office he shared with twenty three other workers.

He quietly passed away on Monday, but nobody noticed until Saturday morning when an office cleaner asked why he was still working on weekend.

George's boss said "George was always the first guy at work each morning and the last to leave at night, so no one found it unusual that he was in the same position all that time and didn't say anything. He was always absorbed in his work and kept to himself."

A post-mortem examination revealed that he had been dead for five days after suffering a heart attack. Ironically, George was proofreading manuscripts of medical textbooks when he died. You may want to give your co-workers a nudge occasionally.

Moral of the story is: Don't work too hard, nobody notices anyway.

*Before leaving his job, Trump asked his manager to write him a recommendation. This is what he wrote.*

## 47. Letter of Recommendation

*To whom it may concern*
*While working with Mr. Trump, I have always found him working studiously and sincerely at his table without gossiping with colleagues in the office. He seldom wastes his time on useless things. Given a job, he always finishes the given assignment in time. He is always deeply engrossed in his official work, and can never be found chitchatting in the canteen. He has absolutely no*

*vanity in spite of his high accomplishment and profound*
*knowledge of his field. I think he can easily be*
*classed as outstanding, and should on no account be*
*dispensed with.I strongly feel that Mr. Trump should be*
*pushed to accept a position, and a proposal to management be*
*sent away as soon as possible.*
A second note following the report:

*Mr. Trump was present when I was writing the report mailed to*
*you today. Kindly read only the alternate lines 1, 3, 5, 7, 9,....... for*
*my true assessment of him.*

*Regards,*
Branch Manager

**After resigning from his position, he had a lot of trouble
finding a new path and tried a lot of different
professions. Here are some of them. First he joined a
Cruise Ship and performed magic tricks to make some
money and this is where he came across the parrot
Twitter for the second time.**

## 48. The Magician and the Parrot

Trump was working on a Cruise Ship in the Caribbean. There was
a different audience each week, so Trump could do the same
tricks over and over again.

There was only one problem, the captain's parrot, Twitter saw the
shows every week and began to understand what the magician did in
every trick. Once he understood that, he started shouting out during
the show.

"Look, it's not the same hat!" "Look, he's hiding the flowers
under the table!" "Hey, why are all the cards the Ace of Spades?"
Trump was furious but couldn't do anything about it; it was the
captain's parrot after all.

One day the ship had an accident and sank. Trump found himself
on a piece of wood, in the middle of the ocean, and of course the
parrot was by his side.

They stared at each other with hatred, but did not utter a word.

This went on for several days.

After a week the parrot finally said, "Okay, I give up. What did you do with the boat?"

*After cashing in his insurance money for his suffering in the accident, he put some of the money in his shoe and was on his way home.*

## 49. Don't search my shoes

Two robbers suddenly attacked Trump and began mugging him. Trump put up a tremendous fight. Finally, the robbers defeated him and took his wallet.

Upon only finding two dollars in his wallet, the surprised robbers exclaimed "Why did you put up such a fight?"

To which Trump promptly replied "I was afraid that you would find the $200 hidden in my shoe."

*The experience of being mugged caused Trump to become disheartened and led to his entry into the world of crime. His goal was to persevere until he had retrieved the equivalent of his $200, but due to his inexperience he always ended up in trouble.*

*Trump convinced his best friend Pence to join him in this new venture and they decided that they would start off by robbing a holiday home.*

## 50. Team player

Trump and Pence smuggled themselves into a very wealthy man's holiday home. They decided to live there for a while. They settled into the roof and came down at night to eat while the owner was away or asleep.

They stayed there for a month and really enjoyed themselves when the owner was out of the country. The owner began to notice, that the food in his fridge was mysteriously disappearing. So he decided to keep an eye on his fridge.

He set a trap to catch whoever was stealing his food. He installed hidden cameras in the house which showed two men coming down from the roof in his living room and eating his food. He decided to surprise them one night. He waited in the darkness for them to come out. They were hungry and started coming down from the roof.

Trump was in the process of going down to eat when all of a sudden a machete hit his arm almost cutting it in half, he made a small muffled squeak and climbed back up into the roof. He then told Pence that he may go first. Pence asked him if anything was wrong. "No nothing is wrong, you go first."

As soon as his friend started descending, the machete hit his arm as well. Only when this happened did Trump cry out in pain. They were both screaming and crying at the same time.

"You are so evil, why didn't you tell me that the man hit you with a machete?" Pence cried out to Trump.

"Well, I couldn't let you get away unscathed while I sit here with half of an arm. We're in this together".

Due to that experience, Pence was no longer keen to accompany Trump in his criminal activity. For his next robbery Trump had to go alone.

*So Trump ventured alone in another suburb.*

## 51. Wake up and come arrest me, I am here to rub you

Trump wanted to rob a house in a complex that had a search light. The search light was not working at the time, but just as he got inside the complex, the search light suddenly came on. He didn't realize this, until he was blinded by the light and thought that he had been seen and was about to be shot at. He screamed out, "Don't shoot, don't shoot" and he fell to the ground, flat on his stomach."

The security guard, who was sleeping, was awoken by the commotion. He realized that there was an intruder in the complex and the thief had already surrendered himself and was lying, face flat, on the ground. All he had to do was put cuffs on Trump and stand him up.

*Trump pleaded his case so well that the guard let him go and made him promise that he would never commit crime again. But Trump did not intend keeping his promise. He attempted a purse snatching but again got caught and had to face the courts for the first time in his life.*

## 52. In a courtroom.

Trump was being questioned.

Q: What is your date of birth?

A: July fifteenth.

Q: What year?

A: Every year.

Trump was sitting on trial for snatching a purse. The victim was describing what happened and had to identify Trump. She said "Yes, that's him, I saw him clear as day and I'd remember his face anywhere." At which point, Trump bursts out "You couldn't see my face, lady, I was wearing a mask!"

*He was released anyway as the prosecution did not have enough evidence to convict him.*
*He got away due to lack of evidence and continued on his path of crime as he had not yet recovered his $200. He tried stealing cars for a change.*

## 53. A Police Cheque

Trump had just crossed a bridge and got stopped by the police. One of the officers walked towards him, smiling and sprinkled flowers on his car. He said

"Congratulations sir! Your car is the one millionth to cross this bridge since it was built two years ago. So for that, we are going to give you a $2000 cheque from the city's projects fund."

Trump very happily replied:

"That is a very good thing, now I will finally be able to buy a driver's license."

Trump's friend emerged out of the car and intervened:

"Don't listen to him officer, he is drunk as a skunk, he doesn't know what he is saying."

At the back of the car, Pence who didn't know what was going on remarked:

"I told you so Trump; we can't go far in a stolen car."

*Trump was arrested for driving a stolen car without a license under the influence of alcohol and was in court once again.*

## 54. When lawyers are part of the jury

The judge was hearing the drunken driving case and Trump, who had both a record and a reputation for driving under the influence, demanded a jury trial. It was nearly four in the afternoon and getting a jury would take time, so the judge called a recess and went out in the hall looking to recruit anyone available for jury duty. He found a dozen lawyers in the main lobby and thought that they would do as a jury. The lawyers thought this would be a novel experience and so followed the judge back to the courtroom.

The trial was over in about ten minutes and it was very clear that Trump was guilty. The jury went into the jury room. After nearly three hours of waiting, the judge was totally out of patience and sent the bailiff into the jury room to see what was holding up the verdict. When the bailiff returned, the judge asked:

"Well have they got a verdict yet?"

The bailiff shook his head and replied:

"Verdict! Hell no! They're still doing nominating speeches for

the foreman's position!"

*The lawyers were in such disagreement that once again Trump was released. He tried once again to get back the $200 that was stolen from him. This time he decided to sell wild lizards to tourists in the Amazon exotic animal Park.*

## 55. Lizard's merchant

Trump was stationed in a zone infested with harmless wild lizards in the park and would tell the tourists visiting that zone, that was selling lizards. That his 'lizards' are genetically modified and that they have a very high IQ as a result of their modification and that they understand English. To prove his point, he would tell a wild lizard in the area that he would be going to a new home; the lizard as always would nod as if in agreement.

When the tourists paid Trump, he would say to lizard "He has paid the money, okay?"

The lizard would nod again, as if in agreement. "He is going to come and get you tomorrow, okay?" Again the lizard would nod his head as it always does

*Obviously the tourists could not get hold of their genetically advanced lizard when they would come to collect it and Trump would be nowhere to be found. So the tourists lodged a complaint against him and he was now wanted by Interpol.*

## 56. Young Monk with mystic powers

Trump ran away to China. He befriended a young monk who had mystical powers. Whenever he and the monk were walking together and Trump was in danger of being apprehended by Interpol, or they were about to go through an enemy zone, the young monk would sing a special song and Trump would be invisible until they crossed the area.

One day, for no apparent reason, Trump was extremely rude to the monk and he insulted the monk so badly that they stopped talking to each other altogether. They had supposedly just got reacquainted when they went for a walk, the Chinese police were coming towards them and the monk started singing, to Trump's surprise, the Chinese headed straight towards him and announced:

"Sir you are under arrest, we have been looking for you for a very long time."

Trump was surprised and kept asking.

"What do you mean, can you see me? Can you really see me?"

*Unfortunately this time he could not avoid prison and was sentenced to serve a couple of years. In prison he contracted all types of sicknesses and became a frequent visitor in the hospital. He called to speak to the doctor, as he lay in his hospital bed.*

## 57. Out of prison in Pieces

"Look here, doctor! You've already removed my spleen, tonsils, adenoids, and one of my kidneys. I asked to speak to you, to find out if you could PLEASE, get me out of this place!"

The doctor replied, "I'm doing it, bit by bit."

*While in hospital, Trump wondered what was wrong with him, as the doctors and nurses were not telling him.*

## 58. How is the patient?

"Hi! Is this reception? I would like to inquire about one of your patients, who is currently in your hospital. I would like to find out if the patient's state is improving or declining"

"What is the name of the patient?

"His name is Trump and he is in room 302" "One moment sir, let me get you the nurse" After a long wait:

"Hi, this is Michelle the nurse, what can I do for you?"

"I would like to know the state of the patient Trump in room 302." "One moment sir, I am going to try to get hold of his doctor" After another long wait:

"Hi, this is Doctor Carson, how can I help you?"

"Hi doctor, I would like to find out about the state of your patient Trump, who has been in the hospital for three weeks now, in room 302" "One moment let me check his file."

After another long wait

"Hummmmm, here it is, he has eaten well today, his blood pressure and pulse are stable, and he is reacting very well to the treatment and we should be able to remove his heart monitor tomorrow. If this continues for the next forty eight hours, he will be allowed to go back to prison."

"AAAhhh! That is wonderful news! I am very happy, thanks" "From the way you took the news, you must surely be a close relative. Are you family?"

"No, this is Trump himself calling from room 302. Everyone is coming in and out of my room and they are not telling me a thing, so I just wanted to find out how I was doing."

*When Trump was released on medical parole, he gave up crime and joined the army and had to do his training.*

## 59. What is that queue for?

A very unpopular drill sergeant had just chewed out Trump, and as he was walking away, he turned to Trump and said "I guess when I die; you'll come and dance on my grave." Trump replied, "Not me, Sarge... no sir! I promised myself that when I get out of the army I'd never stand in another line!"

*After his army training Trump had to complete his shooting training, which he was not very good at.*

## 60. The problem is with the target, if the weapon is firing

He was learning to shoot with a sniper gun. He lay on the ground and aimed at the target and shot continuously.
His sergeant went to check what he hit. He shouted to Trump "No bullets on the target, Trump."
So Trump looked at his gun... and the target... again he looked at his gun... and then the target.
And he put one of his fingers at the end of the barrel and pulled the trigger.
Of course he blew off his finger.
With his finger blown in pieces, Trump screamed to his sergeant:
"Everything is okay this side, I am sure the cause of the problem is over there"

*After his finger recovered, his next exercise was parachute jump training.*

## 61. Full reimbursement in case you don't make it

Trump was going to try his first parachute jump that day.
The instructor explained:
"It is very easy, you get in the plane and when I say go, you jump, then, you pull this string and the parachute will open. You will come down without a problem."
"And what if the parachute doesn't work?" asked Trump.
"Well, we have full guarantees on all our parachutes. Just bring the parachute back to me and I'll return it to the supplier"

*Now that Trump's training was over, world war X just started and Trump was about to be deployed.*

## 62. Small groups of two million

The Chinese had decided to invade Taiwan to prevent America's influence on the region.
The Chinese general said to his troops, "We are going to cross the border by means of small groups of two or three million people."

*Before leaving for battle, the inexperienced soldier Trump realized that he did not have a rifle, so he went to his commander and told him that he did not have a rifle.*

## 63. What Weapon is the enemy using?

"That's no problem, son" said the sergeant. "Here, take this broom. Just point it at the enemy, and say 'Bangety Bang Bang'"

"But what about a bayonet, Sarge?" asked Trump.

The sergeant pulled a piece of straw from the end of the broom, and attached it to the handle end. "Here, use this... just go, 'Stabity Stab Stab'."

Trump ended up alone on the battlefield, holding just his broom. Suddenly, the enemy soldier charged at him.

Trump pointed the broom at the soldier: "Bangety Bang Bang" he shouted. The enemy fell dead. More enemies appeared. Trump, amazed at his good luck, shouted "Bangety Bang Bang, Stabity Stab Stab." He mowed down the enemy by the dozen.

Finally, the battlefield was clear, except for one soldier who was walking slowly towards him. "Bangety Bang Bang" shouted Trump. The soldier kept coming towards him.

"Bangety Bang Bang," repeated Trump, but to no avail. He got desperate. "Bangety Bang Bang, Stabity Stab Stab."

It's was no use. The enemy kept coming. He stomped Trump onto

the ground, and shouted "Tankety Tank Tank."

*He miraculously survived again and was brought back home and promoted to Sergeant. He was invited on a radio talk show to speak about the army, the war and his new recruits.*

## 64. Equipped to be a prostitute

Lady interviewer: "So, Sergeant Trump, what kind of training are you going to give these young boys?"

Sergeant Trump: "We're going to teach them climbing, fighting, swimming, and shooting."

Lady interviewer: "Shooting! That's a bit irresponsible, isn't it?"

Sergeant Trump: "I don't see why, they'll be properly supervised on the training camp."

Lady interviewer: "Don't you admit that this is a terribly

dangerous activity to be teaching new recruits?"

Sergeant Trump: "I don't see why, we will be teaching them proper discipline before they even touch a firearm."
Lady interviewer: "But you're equipping them to become violent killers."
Sergeant Trump: "Well, you're equipped to be a prostitute, but you're not one, are you?"

*After the war, Trump was traumatized and resigned from the army; he found a job in the local flea market.*

## 65. Why are you still laughing?

On one occasion, he farted loudly while working at the flea market. Everybody in the market laughed, which embarrassed him greatly. A while after the incident, Trump went back to his stall, he came out and saw a woman who had a big smile on her face. Trump became very angry with her and beat her up. He then went back to his stall. He later came out to see if the woman was still smiling. "Are you still smiling out here?" He asked the woman.

When he saw that she was, he beat her up again and went back into his stall.

A little later, he came back out and saw that she was still smiling; this made him want to beat her up again. This is when the people in the flea market intervened and stopped him:

"NO, no, her face always looks like she is smiling" they said.
Trump realized his mistake and apologized to the poor lady.

*After the incident, the woman complained to the flea market owners. He lost his job but found another job as a ranger through the help of his friend Pence who was now working at an animal park.*

## 66. Let's eat them before the mating begins

A Russian scientist and a French scientist had spent their lives studying the grizzly bear. Each year they petitioned their respective governments to allow them to go to Northern Park to study the bears. Finally their request was granted, and they immediately flew to the Park.

They reported to the ranger station. Trump told them that it was the grizzly mating season and it was too dangerous to go out and study the animals. They pleaded that this was their only chance and finally Trump relented. The Russian and the French were given portable phones and told to report in every day. For several days they called in, and then nothing was heard from the two scientists. Trump and Pence mounted a search party and found the camp completely ravaged with no sign of the missing men. They followed the trail of a male and a female bear. They found the female and decided they must kill the animal to find out if she had eaten the scientist because they feared an international incident. They killed the female animal and opened the stomach to find the remains of the Russian. Trump turned to Pence and said, "You know what this means, don't you?" Pence responded: "Of course, the French is in the male."

*After that incident, he resigned from the Park and relocated to America where he got a job as a cowboy on a ranch. He went to a bar where some of his peers met.*

## 67. You left your horse's engine on

Trump and an Indian ex-colleague from the ranch, walked into a bar one day and sat down to drink a beer.

After a few minutes, a big tall cowboy walked in and said:
"Who owns the big white horse outside?"

Trump stood up, hitched his gun belt, and said "I do. Why?"

The cowboy looked at Trump and said, "I just thought you would like to know that your horse is almost dead!"

Trump and the Indian rushed outside and sure enough, the horse was almost dead from heat exhaustion. Trump got him some water and soon the horse was starting to feel a little better.

Trump turned to his Indian friend and said: "I want you to run around Silver and see if you can create enough of a breeze to make him feel better."

His Indian friend said "Sure Trump", and began running circles around Silver. Not able to do anything else but wait, Trump returned to the bar to finish his drink.

A few minutes later, another cowboy strutted into the bar and asked: "Who owns that big white horse outside?"

Trump jumped up again and claimed, "I do. What is wrong with him this time?"

The cowboy answered "Nothing much, I just wanted you to know, you left your engine running."

## 68. Let's eat his nuts

Trump had never been hunting before, while Pence had hunted on numerous occasions. When they got to the Kouncy woods, Pence told Trump to sit by a tree and not make a sound while he checked out a deer stand. After he got about a quarter of a mile away, Pence heard a blood-curdling scream. He rushed back to Trump and yelled "I thought I told you to be quiet!" Trump said "Hey, I tried. I really did. When those snakes crawled over me, I didn't make a sound.

When that bear was breathing down my neck, I didn't make a peep. But when those two chipmunks crawled up my pants leg and said 'Should we take them with us or eat them here? I couldn't be quiet any longer!"

*They went on with the hunting and there was an incident where it appeared that Trump had died.*

## 69. Make sure he is dead before we can help

Trump and Pence continued hunting deep into the forest when Trump suddenly fell unconscious. He seemed to have stopped breathing and his eyes were all white.

Pence panicked and called 911. "My friend is dead! What can I do?" The operator calmly replied "calm down sir. I can help you. First we need to make sure he is dead."

There was a moment of silence and then a loud gunshot was heard.

"Okay, now what must I do?" said Pence

*Fortunately he missed his target and the loud bang woke Trump up.*

## 70. What was he doing in the maid's room?

After hunting, Trump stopped at his local bar, Mammy's, for a drink. He had the bad habit of clumsily throwing his gun down onto the counter, sometimes hitting the head. Mammy always warned him that one day, he would forget to take the bullets out and a catastrophe would occur.

The next day Trump came in and threw his gun on the counter.
A shot fired up through the ceiling.
"See" said Mammy, "I told you not to throw your gun down like that! Today the barmaid was not feeling well and I sent her upstairs to lie down in her room, which is directly above here. I can't even bring myself to see what has happened. You go!!!"
Trump went upstairs, he returned and cheerfully said:
"All is well! The maid was lying on her bed, her legs wide open and the bullet passed directly between her legs without scratching her." "Phew" said Mammy! "That was a miracle."
"Yeah" said Trump, but your husband's head is all over the roof."

*Trump had grown into quite a tough character, due to his experience as a ranger and his experience as a sergeant in the army, he wanted to show off when he went into a bar for a drink.*

## 71. My name is Bill. Which bill?

Trump went on a trip to the Far East. He walked into a bar that he knew from his first visit to the region.
Trump called to the barman
"Look here."
He threw a coin into the air and with his gun, shot a whole in it. Then he said:
"My name is Bill, Buffalo Bill."
The barman pulled down his pants and said "Look at this!"
Trump noticed he had two penises and six balls. The barman exclaimed:
"My name is also Bill, Tcherno Bill"

*The next day Trump went back to the same bar. He finished his drink and left the bar only to notice that someone had stolen his horse. He came back to find the thief.*

## 72. My horse or I will do what I did at Carson City

"Who took my horse? Answer! Or I will do what I did at Carson City!"
There was silence in the bar and the atmosphere was filled

with tension.

"I am warning you again! Where is my horse? Or I will do what I did at Carson City."

The people in the bar were trembling with fear. Just then the person who took the horse owned up out of fear of what Trump would do and returned Trump's horse to him. Trump was now satisfied. "Okay, I'm going now" said Trump.

The barman asked him out of curiosity:

"So Trump, what happened at Carson City?"

"Nothing, I went home walking"

*Now once again, Trump tried his hand at fishing and he went on an escapade with Pence and they got lost. This is where they met Djinna the genie, for the first time.*

## 73. The Genie Djinna

Trump and Pence were lost at sea in their boat. After many days of navigating, without eating a thing for five days and nothing to drink for two days, they saw a lamp floating in the sea. They picked it up and while cleaning it, a genie called Djinna appeared. Pence remarked with surprise "this genie is very old"

The genie replied "Listen guys, you have freed me from this lamp and I am very grateful, I usually make three of your wishes come true but I am too old for that; so I will make only one of your wishes come true. So think carefully before deciding on your wish. Without thinking Trump said:

"We wish to have enough beer to drink for the rest of our lives." As soon as he said that, the genie transformed the ocean into beer and disappeared. Pence turned toward him and slapped him behind the head.

"Well done Einstein, now we will have to pee in the boat."

*They finally ended up on an island and were captured by some Aborigines. There was another prisoner there, who had been captured previously. The three intruders where to be punished by the chief*

## 74. Death or Booka

The first explorer was called to stand in front of the tribe and was asked: "Death or Booka?"

The first explorer did not want to die, so he opted for 'Booka.' The tribe started screaming 'BOOKA!' and dancing around. The chief then ripped the explorer's pants off and sodomized him. The chief then called Pence to the front and asked "Death or Booka?" Not wanting to die either, he opted for 'Booka.' The tribe again started screamed 'BOOKA!' and dancing around. The chief ripped Pence's pants off and sodomized him.

The chief called Trump to the front and asked "Death or Booka?" Trump had a little more self respect and thought death would be better than being violated in front of hundreds of tribesman, so he opted for death. The chief turned to the tribe and screamed "DEATH BY BOOKA!"

*Booka could not kill him though, so they let him go. He then tried coaching for a while but was hired in a school were the principal, the students and the teachers were all dumb.*

## 75. Go over to my office and see if I am there

Trump was now a basketball coach at a university. He wanted a salary increase, so he stormed into the Principal's office and demanded a raise, right there and then.

"Please" protested the Principal, "you already earn more money than the entire history department."

"Yeah, maybe so, but you don't know what I have to put up with" Trump blustered, "Look."

He went out into the hall and grabbed a student who was jogging down the hallway. He said to him:

"Run over to my office and see if I'm there" he ordered.

Twenty minutes later the student returned, sweaty and out of breath.

"You're not there, sir" he reported.

"Oh, I see what you mean" conceded the Principal, scratching his head.

"I would have phoned first."

*Trump is now a security guard at a University. The university was testing a fascinating diagnostic computer which could help diagnose the health of a large number of people quickly and easily.*

## 76. Diagnostic Computer

In line at the university cafeteria, Trump said to the principal behind him:

"You know, my damn elbow hurts like hell! I guess I better see a doctor."

"Listen my friend, you don't have to spend that kind of money," the principal replied. "There's a diagnostic computer at the pharmacy at the corner. Just give it a urine sample and the computer will tell you what's wrong and what to do about it. It only takes ten seconds and costs ten dollars... a hell of a lot cheaper than a doctor!"

So Trump took a urine sample in a small jar and took it to the pharmacy. He put ten dollars in the machine and the computer lit up and asked for the urine sample. He poured the sample into the slot and waited.

Ten seconds later, the computer ejected a printout; you have tennis elbow. Soak your arm in warm water and avoid heavy activity. It will improve in two weeks. WOW! AWESOME! He was blown away! That evening while thinking how amazing this new technology was, Trump began wondering if the computer could be fooled. Hmmmm......... So he proceeded to mix some tap water, a stool sample from his dog, urine samples from his wife and daughter and masturbated into the mixture for good measure!

Trump hurried back to the pharmacy, eager to check the results. He deposited ten dollars, poured in his concoction, and awaited the results. The computer printed the following:

1. Your tap water is too hard. Get a water softener.
2. Your dog has ringworm. Bathe him with anti-fungal shampoo.
3. Your daughter has a cocaine habit. Get her into rehab.
4. Your wife is pregnant... twin girls. They aren't yours. Get a lawyer.
5. And, if you don't stop playing with yourself, your damn elbow will never get better!

*This experience with the machine motivated him to study medicine. After many years of studying he became a Doctor.*

## 77. New and second hand brain

In the Hospital where he worked, the relatives of a gravely ill family member gathered in the waiting room. Finally, Doctor Trump came in looking tired.

"I'm afraid I am the bearer of bad news" he said as he surveyed their worried faces.

"The only hope left for your loved one at this time is a brain transplant. It's an experimental procedure, semi-risky, and you will have to pay for the brain yourselves."

The family members sat silently as they absorbed the news. After a long time, someone asked, "Well, how much does a brain cost?"

Trump quickly responded "$5000 for a male brain, and $200 for a female brain."

The moment turned awkward. Men in the room tried not to smile, avoiding eye contact with the women, but some actually smirked.

A man, unable to control his curiosity, blurted out the question everyone wanted to ask,

"Why is the male brain so much more?"

Trump smiled at the entire group said:

"It's just standard pricing procedure. We have to mark down

the price of the female brains, because they've been used."

*A man just ran into a hospital needing urgent help.*

## 78. What type of labor is she in?

A man rushed into the ER at the hospital and shouted,

"My wife's going to have her baby in the taxi!"

Trump grabbed his equipment, rushed out to the taxi, lifted the lady's dress, and began to take off her underwear.

Suddenly he noticed that there were several taxis, and he was in

the wrong one.

*Trump was examining an elderly woman in his consulting rooms.*

## 79. Big breaths or big breasts?

At the beginning of his shift Trump placed a stethoscope on an elderly and slightly deaf female patient's anterior chest wall. "Big breaths" he instructed.

"Yes, they used to be" remorsefully replied the patient.

## 80. Gynecologist's funeral

His colleague used to be a very famous cardiac surgeon; many of his peers were present.

He was buried in a crypt. At the entrance, the door of the vault had been adorned with a big 6 feet high heart, made with flowers and the casket was put inside. After the final farewell, the gigantic heart opened up and the casket was placed inside and then the heart was closed.

Everyone was silent and amazed by this demonstration.

Suddenly, Trump began to laugh out loud.

Pence, who was sitting next to him, reprimanded him with a severe look.

"Be quiet, what's got into you to laugh like that?"

"I was just thinking of my own funeral as I am a gynecologist!"

*He returned to the hospital to find that one of his*
*patients could not remember where he was.*

## 81. You lost your legs and we have a buyer for your shoes

Patient: I'm in a hospital! Why am I in here?

Trump: You've had an accident involving a bus.

Patient: What happened?

Trump: Well, I've got some good news and some bad news. Which would you like to hear first?

Patient: Give me the bad news first.

Trump: Your legs were injured so badly that we had to amputate both of them.

Patient: That's terrible! What's the good news?

Trump: There's a guy in the next ward who made a very good

offer on your shoes.

*Due to unprofessional practices, he was barred from*
*being a gynecologist and he decided to study further to*
*become a dentist.*

## 82. Scare my patients off, I have an appointment

Newly qualified as a dentist, Trump had just completed work on a patient; he then said to the patient:

"Could you help me? Could you give out a few of your loudest, most painful screams?"

"Why? Doctor, it wasn't all that bad this time" replied the patient.

"There are so many people in the waiting room right now, and I don't want to miss the four o'clock Golf" explained Trump.

*At the time when Trump was a dentist, he met his Chinese friend Fu, for the first time, Fu just arrived from China.*

## 83. Chinese Toothache

At ten o'clock in the morning, the phone rang at Trump's office "Hello!" said Trump.

"Hello!" said Fu, "What time you fixee teeth for me?" "Two-thirty, alright? Asked Trump

"Yes," said Fu. "Tooth hurtee, alright! But what time you fixee?"

*Trump found dentistry boring so he decided to try pharmacy instead. When he qualified he got a job in a pharmacy.*

## 84. I need to poison my husband. Do you have a prescription?

A lady walked into the pharmacy where Trump was working and told him that she needed some cyanide. Trump responded "Why in the world do you need cyanide?" The lady then explained that she needed it to poison her husband. Trump's eyes widened as he responded "Lord have mercy, I can't give you cyanide to kill your husband! That's against the law! They'll throw both of us in jail and I'll lose my license."

The lady then reached into her purse and pulled out a picture of her husband in bed with Trump's wife and handed it to him. Trump looked at the picture and replied:

"Well now, you didn't tell me you had a prescription."

*Trump soon became bored with pharmacy and enrolled to study psychiatry due to his fascination with the human mind. He qualified after few years of study.*

### 85. I know it's wrong but I can't keep a secret

While attending a psychiatry convention, Trump and two other psychiatrists took a walk. "People are always coming to us with their guilt and fears" said the one, "but we have no one to go to with our own problems."

"Since we're all professionals" Trump suggested, "why don't we hear each other out right now?" They agreed this was a good idea. The first psychiatrist confessed "I'm a compulsive shopper and I am deeply in debt, so I usually overcharge my patients as often as I can." The second admitted "I have a drug problem that's out of control, and I frequently pressure my patients into buying illegal drugs for me."

Then Trump said "I know it's wrong, but no matter how hard I try,

I just can't keep a secret."

*A patient made him think maybe treating people was not the right profession for him.*

### 86. Doctor, I think someone is under my bed

A patient went to Trump for help.

"Doctor, I have a problem. Every night, when I am on my bed, I have a weird feeling that someone is hiding under my bed. Then I stand up and look under the bed, and of course, there is no one. I go back and after a while I tell myself maybe I didn't check properly and stand up to check again and this goes on the whole night. I tell myself I am being paranoid, but I always feel the need to check that there is no one under the bed. Doctor, all this is ruining my life, can you do something to help me?"

"Oh... I see... obsessive compulsive..., It's going to take four years of treatment, three sessions a week and you will be cured of your obsession" said Trump

"Doctor, how much is it's going cost?" asked the patient

"Well, $60 per session. $180 a month, $2160 a year, so $8700 in total" replied Trump

"Wow... I will think about it ..." said the patient

A month passed by and Trump saw the patient walking down the street.

"So why didn't you come for the treatment?" asked Trump.

"$8700 was a bit high. A pizza delivery guy solved my problem for $30."

"What did he do?"

"He told me to cut off the bed's legs"

*Trump decided to try plumbing for a change.*

## 87. I have a PhD and I don't charge that much

Trump qualified as a plumber and was attending to a leaking faucet at a neurosurgeon's house. After a two-minute job, Trump demanded $150.

The neurosurgeon exclaimed, "I don't charge that much an hour, even though I am a surgeon."

Trump replied "I agree; you are right."

When I was a surgeon, I didn't charge that much either. That's why

I switched to plumbing!"

*Trump decided to try his hand at photography for a while, this is where he met Fu again.*

## 88. Where is my ID photo?

His friend Fu and a group of his Chinese friends were his first clients. They wanted to have ID photo's taken. Trump was finding the whole exercise very monotonous. By the tenth person, who happened to be Fu, Trump decided to give them all the same picture, to make things easier.

When it was time to collect the pictures, Fu arrived and Trump gave him his picture.

"That's not me" said Fu.

"What do you mean, is this not your face?"

"It's my face but not my shirt!"

*Trump did not enjoy being a photographer. He decided that he would give construction work a try.*

## 89. I bet you a pack of beer that you are

Trump, Pence and Pen were doing some construction work together. At their lunch break, they were sitting on a scaffold eating their lunch. All of a sudden, the whole structure shook and Ken fell off and died.

The two survivors realized that one of them would have to tell Ken's family about the unfortunate event.

Pence volunteered as he was good at handling this kind of situation. He went to his friend Ken's house to break the bad news and returned to the construction site with a pack of cold drinks.

"Look, I brought us some drinks," he said.

"Didn't you go to Ken's wife?" asked Trump, worried.

"Of course I did" replied Pence.

"Where did you get that pack of drinks from?" asked Trump.

"Ken's wife gave it to me" said Pence.

Trump was confused.

"You told her, that her husband had passed away and she gave you a pack of drinks? Tell me what happened"

"I went there, rang the bell and asked if the widow of Ken stays here."

"No, she said, you must be mistaken, I am not a widow" "And I said"

"I bet you a pack of beer that you are."

*The next day at lunchtime; Trump, Pence and Ken's replacement tried to kill themselves over their lunch.*

## 90. I work this hard and have to eat crap

The next day, at lunchtime Trump, Pence and the new guy were about to eat their lunch.

The new guy opened his lunch box and said "Eeew, turkey! I hate turkey!" So he shot himself with a rivet gun.

Pence opened his lunch box and said "Eeew, ham! I hate ham!" So he jumped off the building.

Trump opened his box and said "Eeew, mac and cheese! I hate mac and cheese!" So he ran himself over with a bulldozer.

At the hospital waiting room, their three wives were talking about their husbands. The first two were very sad, but the third was rather puzzled.

The first wife said "I thought he liked turkey!"

The second one said "I thought he liked ham!"
But Trump's wife was still puzzled. She said "He packed his

own lunch."

*Few days after their discharge from hospital, Pence was run over by a driver under the influence and the driver has to appear in court. Trump was*
*giving evidence about the accident he had witnessed.*

## 91. I knew an idiot would ask me that

The lawyer of the victim asked him how far away he was from
the accident.
Trump replied "7 feet, 5 and half inches" he replied.
"What? How come you are so sure of that distance?" asked
the lawyer.
"I knew sooner or later some idiot would ask me. So I measured

it!" replied Trump.

*Due to his offensive replies in the court that day, he was charged with contempt of court and was sentenced never to practice carpentry again. He now decided to become a fire-fighter.*

## 92. Use the cat's testicles as a siren

Trump was working on the engine outside the fire station when he
noticed a little girl next door in a little red wagon with little ladders
hung off of the side and a garden hose tightly coiled in the middle.
The girl was wearing a fire-fighter's helmet and had the wagon
tied to a dog and a cat. Trump walked over to take a closer look.
"That sure is a nice fire truck" Trump said, with admiration.
"Thanks" the little girl said. Trump looked a little closer and
noticed the girl has tied the wagon to the dog's collar and to the
cat's testicles.
"Little girl" Trump said "I don't want to tell you how to run your
fire truck, but if you were to tie that rope around the cat's collar, I
think you would go faster." The little girl said:
"You're probably right, but then I wouldn't have a siren.

### 93. Made in Japan

A Japanese tourist arrived in town and took Trump's taxi, to go see the Taj tour. In the taxi, looking through the window, he saw a motorbike overtaking the taxi and tapped on Trump's shoulder and said:

"Moto Kawasaki, very fast, made in Japan."

After a while a car overtook the taxi and again the Japanese tourist tapped Trump on the shoulder and said "that Toyota car, very fast, made in Japan."

Once they reached their destination, Trump said:

"Here we are. The price is $150."

The Japanese tourist was shocked by the high price and remarked: "ehhhhhh ... very expensive!"

Trump said with a smile:

"Oh yes, very fast, made in Japan."

*Another overseas passenger got into Trump's taxi.*

### 94. The trip is worth $35

The ride cost $30, but the tourist did not have enough money to pay him. He said to Trump:

"I only have $30; can you go back the equivalent of $5 and drop me there?"

*Of course Trump went back and dropped him where the ride would have cost $25 and now has just picked up a French customer.*

### 95. A French man in town

A man from France got into Trump's Mercedes Benz taxi. Intrigued, he asked Trump what the signs in front of the car meant (the Mercedes sign). Trump said it is to aim at the people walking in the street and to show the Frenchman, he pretended to target someone and avoided him inches before contact. At the same time, he heard a loud "boom"!

The Frenchman then said "you would have missed him, if I didn't open the door!"

*Trump was now tired of all these career changes and began to show signs of mental fatigue; he took a break from being a taxi driver and decided to look for a job as a Shopkeeper.*

## 96. What do you sell here?

Trump walked into a doughnut shop and asked for a job, the manager decided to give Trump a test. So he walked out of the shop and came back in, pretending to be a customer.

Manager: What do you sell here?

Trump: Uh... I dunno.

Manager: No, you've got to say "Doughnuts"

So the manager went out and came back in again.

Manager: What do you sell here?

Trump: Uhhh... Doughnuts!

Manager: Are they fresh?

Trump: Uh... I dunno.

Manager: No, you've got to say "Yes, yes, very fresh"

Again he walked out of the shop and re-entered.

Manager: What do you sell here?

Trump: Doughnuts!

Manager: Are they fresh?

Trump: Uh... Yes, yes, very fresh!

Manager: Can I have one?

Trump: Uh... I dunno.

Manager: No, no, no, you've got to say "If you don't, then someone else will."

So the manager walked out and came back in AGAIN.

Manager: What do you sell here?

Trump: Doughnuts!

Manager: Are they fresh?

Trump: Yes, yes, very fresh!

Manager: Can I have one?

Trump: If you don't, then somebody else will!

So he got the job. On his first day of work, a guy came in with a 9mm gun in his pocket.

Guy: What's in the cash register?

Trump: Doughnuts!

Guy: Are you being fresh with me?

Trump: Yes, yes, very fresh!

The guy took a gun out of his pocket and held it up to Trump's head. Guy: Do you want me to blow your brains out?
Trump: If you don't, somebody else will!

*Luckily the guy did not shoot him but Trump was eventually fired for being so dim. Before leaving the shop, a blind man visited the shop and he was looking around.*

## 97. My dog is looking around for me

An old blind man and his Seeing Eye dog walked into Trump's doughnut store.
When he walked in, he started swinging his dog around by the tail. Trump was upset by this and demanded to know why he was doing this.
The blind man calmly replied "I'm just looking around."

*Trump wanted to get rich now, so he decided to try his luck at the casino.*

## 98. Revenge

He lost all his money at the casino. He didn't even have enough money for a taxi to take him to his hotel.
He tried to negotiate a trip back to his hotel but the only taxi driver available refused to help him out.
"No money, no taxi!" said the taxi driver.
"I will send you a cheque as soon as I get home" said Trump.
The taxi driver refused and as this was the only taxi around, he decided to walk to his hotel.
Six months later, Trump bought the book "how to become a millionaire" He followed the book's advice and become rich. He went back to the casino and he made a small fortune gambling that day. Leaving the casino, he saw a long queue of taxis and right at the end, he saw the taxi that previously refused to give him a lift.
He got into the first taxi and said to the driver:
"I would like to go back to my hotel, but on our way, I would like you to stop and give me a BJ."
The taxi driver was furious and stopped and threw him out.
He got into the second taxi and said. "I would like to go back to my

hotel, but on our way, I would like you to stop and give me a BJ."
The driver insulted him and threw him out.
Trump was not discouraged and continued with his proposition to
the rest of the taxis in the line and they all threw him out.
He then got into the taxi that had refused him the lift and asked him
to take him to his hotel.
As the taxi driver drove past all the other taxis in the queue, all the
other taxi drivers looked at the taxi driver in disgust.
Trump just gave a big smile and a wink.

*Trump told Pence about the book 'How To Become A
Millionaire' the one that helped him get become rich.
Pence wanted to borrow it, so that he could become a
millionaire too.*

## 99. How to make a million or at least half a million

Trump gave him the book but half the pages were missing.
On seeing Pence's disappointed face, Trump remarked:
- What's the matter? Isn't half a million enough for you?

*Trump bought a sports car and was enjoying driving it
on the freeway. He was soon pulled over by a cop.*

## 100. Police Check

"Sir, can I see you drivers license please?"
"I don't have it anymore. It got suspended months ago after
five major infractions."
"Can I see the car's papers?"
"I don't know, it is not my car, I just stole
it." "This car is stolen?"
"Yeah, come to think of it, I think I saw some papers in the
cubby hole when I was putting my gun away."
"So there is a gun in the cubby hole of this car?"
"Yes sir, I put it there when I killed the woman who owned the
car." "You killed the owner of the car?"
"Yes sir. The body is in the boot"
"The body is in the boot?"
"Yes sir."
The police man stepped backward, took out his radio and called for

backup. They got there as quickly as they could and circled around the car. An officer approached the car and asked Trump:

"Can I see your papers sir?"

"Here" said Trump

The papers were in order.

"Can I see the car's papers sir?"

Trump opened the cubby hole, pulled the car papers out and presented them to the police.

"So you don't have a weapon?" asked the police looking inside the cubby hole."

"No sir"

"Step slowly outside the car without any sudden movements and open the boot."

Trump opened the boot and it was empty. "So you don't have a body in the car?" "No sir"

"It was reported to me that you don't have a license and you had a gun in the car which you used to steal this car and kill its owner, whose body you put in the boot of the car."

"I suppose the guy who told you that also told you that I

was speeding!"

> *Trump, who was now wealthy, wanted to do something for his community, so he became a priest and invested his money into a new church. He appointed himself as the Minister. He had to start making a profit so He devised a plan.*

## 101. The church is full

Trump stood at the pulpit of his church and announced what the sermon for the following Sunday would be about: "To stick, to penetrate, to discharge and to enjoy."

"See you next Sunday" he said.

Rumors of the sermon spread during the week. The next Sunday, the church was so full that they even had rows of people standing at the back.

After a lucrative collection of donations from the crowd, Trump came up to the pulpit and said:

"Stick into your heads that to penetrate in the kingdom of heaven,

You will have to be discharged of your sins so you will enjoy

an eternal paradise."

*Unfortunately that sermon was a disappointment. After that day, church attendance numbers dropped drastically, as well as donations. The Bishop came to visit Trump's new church for the first time.*

## 102. When the priest and his maid were tempted

While visiting the church, the Bishop noticed that there was only one bed in the single room of the church. He asked Trump:

"You only have one bed in your church?"

"Yes, bishop, we are too poor to afford another bed."

"What about your maid, where does she sleep?"

"On the bed, we have a big dog, which is very well behaved and it sleeps between the two of us."

"Surely you are tempted from time to time. What do you do then?"

"When it happens, I get up and go for a walk in the church and when I feel alright I return."

"What about your maid?" she must get tempted from time to time.

"When that happens, she gets up and goes for a walk too" "What happens then when both of you are tempted?"

"In that case, bishop, we send the dog for a walk around the church."

*Trump gave his maid a lesson in grammar.*

## 103. Grammar lesson in the church

Trump's maid said "Father, our alter wine has
arrived!" He replied,

"Sister, it's not our alter wine as you don't have the right to drink it. So you have to say your wine. Do you understand?"

The next day the sister said again "Father, your wood for heating the church has arrived."

"Sister, you must say our wood to heat the church, as we both use it! Do you understand? Is that all Sister?"

"No father" replied the Sister "your zip is open and OUR stick is out hanging"

*The next Sunday's sermon was even more catastrophic, as*

## 104. The Sermon

Trump spoke eloquently during the offertory prayer. He began, with arms extended towards heaven and a rapturous look on his upturned face, "Without you we are but dust"
He would have continued but at that moment someone's daughter in the congregation, who had been listening attentively, leaned over to her mother and asked quite audibly in her shrill little girl voice "Mom, what is Butt Dust?"

*Trump was now broke and the church was on the verge of bankruptcy, he desperately needed money. He got a chance to make some money at an unusual funeral.*

## 105. The priest and his Neighbor

The church was next door to a very rich man. The man had a dog that he loved very much. One day he came back from work, only to find his dog was dead. He started calling loudly for help.
Trump heard him call and came to see what had happened.
The rich man asked him to pray for the dog to rest in peace. Trump categorically refused and told the man that he only prayed for people. The man stood silent for a while then he put his hand in his pocket and placed a wad of cash in Trump's pocket. He then repeated his initial request.
Trump whispered in the rich man's ear "Why didn't you tell me the dog was a Christian?" Prayers were performed

*The church eventually went bankrupt and Trump was forced to change his career.*

## 106. The priest and the magical frog

Trump was crossing the road when a frog called to him and said: "If you kiss me, I will transform into a magnificent princess." He picked up the frog and put it in his pocket.

Again the frog said:

"If you kiss me, I will transform in a magnificent princess and will stay with you for a week."

Trump took the frog out of his pocket, looked at it, smiled and then put it back.

Again the frog repeated:

"If you kiss me, I will transform into a magnificent princess, stay with you for a week and do whatever you want."

Again, Trump took the frog out of his pocket, looked at it, smiled and then put it back.

The frog now irritated, asked angrily:

"What's wrong? I am telling you, I am a princess and I will stay with you for a week and do whatever you want, so why aren't you kissing me?"

Trump replied,

"Look at me, I am a priest and I am not allowed to have a

girlfriend but a talking frog is cool."

*Being an priest was too stressful and not very lucrative for the ex-millionaire Trump. So he decided to become a politician as there was plenty of easy money there, to be made.*

*With his rich career and experience, Trump decided that he would become a politician. He took on his political name 'MAGA'. He had to promise something major to create the excitement and attract the attention of the crowd that he had gathered:*

## 107. We are going to the Sun at night

MAGA was addressing his followers during an election campaign rally.

"We have already gone to the moon and came back. I will show you real technology when I am elected; we will go to the sun and come back."

A foreign journalist approached him when he was leaving the stage and whispered to him:

"Sir, if you go to the sun you will be grilled like a chicken."

MAGA replied "We will go there at night, bitch."

## 108. Be careful what you wish for, your enemy is going to get double

Trump was walking along the beach shortly after he started his political career. On the beach he found a can, the can looked full. He picked it up and opened it out of curiosity and all of a sudden, the genie Djinna appeared and said: "I have been trapped in this can since our last meeting and you have freed me, so I am going to make true three of your wishes, but be careful, whatever you ask for, your worst enemy will get the double of what you get."

Trump thought for a while and said: "I want to be a billionaire."

"Okay, but remember your worst enemy will be twice as rich as you."

Trump then said: "I would like to have the ten most beautiful models in the world at my feet."

"Okay, done, what is your last wish?"

"Well, to top it all off, I would like you to remove one of my testicles."

*In case you never guessed who his enemy was, here is a hint: A rich politician who has no balls.*

*MAGA, also known as 'Trump', was now the president and people were coming to realize that all the promises he made were not being fulfilled and that the trip to the sun was not for this presidential term or this lifetime.*

*People were beginning to hate him and even people who saved his life were afraid to talk about it.*

## 109. I need to arrange a funeral, my father is going to kill me

Three Children saved MAGA from drowning. To thank them, he asked them what would make them happy.

The first one said, a Play Station 4, as he couldn't afford it.

The second one said, a bike, as he couldn't afford it.

The third one asked for a nice funeral.

MAGA asked "But why do you want a funeral while you are still alive?"

"Because my dad will kill me when he finds out that I saved

YOU from drowning."

*MAGA hired his Chinese friend Fu and a jew son in law as advisors.*

## 110. The Chinese and the Jew

Jarred, the Jewish and Fu, the Chinese where onboard the airforce 1.
It was the first time they had flown together and it was obvious
by the silence between them, that they didn't get along.
After thirty minutes, Jarred spoke "I don't like the Chinese."
Fu replied, "Ooooh, no like Chinese? Why ees that?"
Jarred said, "You bombed Pearl Harbor. That's why I don't like the Chinese."
Fu said "Noooo, noooo.... Chinese not bomb Pearl Harbah. That Japanese do, not Chinese."
Jarred answered, "Chinese, Japanese, Vietnamese... what's the difference, they're all the same.
Another thirty minutes of silence passed.
Finally Fu said "I no like Jews."
Jarred replied: "Why not? Why don't you like Jews?"
Fu replied "Jews sink Titanic."
Jarred corrected him "No, no. The Jews didn't sink the Titanic. It was an iceberg."
Fu replied: "Iceberg, Goldberg, Rosenberg, no mattah, All same same."

*Trump was flying in the presidential plane with Pence who was now known as VP and in politics they were didn't get along. At least that's what they wanted the people to believe.*

## 111. If I throw one note, I will make one person happy

MAGA and VP were in the plane on a flight.

VP said,

"I could throw a $100 note out the window and make someone

happy."

MAGA said, "I can throw ten of them and make ten people happy.

Then the pilot said to his co-pilot, do you hear these two arrogant people, they don't realize I can throw two idiots through the window and make 300000000 people happy.

*They were going to the world economic forum and due to the global crisis; they decided to share a plane with some famous people.*

## 112. Where is the world's smartest man?

The airforce one was flying to the World Economic Forum. There were five people on board, the pilot, Mayweather, Bill Gates, MAGA and VP. Suddenly, an illegal oxygen generator exploded loudly in the luggage compartment, and the passenger taxi began to fill with smoke. The cockpit door opened, and the pilot burst into the compartment. "Gentlemen" he began, "I have good news and bad news. The bad news is that we're about to crash in Switzerland. The good news is that there are four parachutes, and I have one of them!" With that, the pilot threw open the door and jumped from the plane. Mayweather was on his feet in a flash. "Gentlemen" he said "I am the world's greatest athlete. The world needs great athletes. I think the world's greatest athlete should have a parachute!" With these words, he grabbed one of the remaining parachutes and hurtled through the door and into the night.

Bill Gates rose and said "Gentlemen, I am the world's smartest man. The world needs smart men. I think the world's smartest man should have a parachute too." He grabbed one, and out he jumped. MAGA and VP looked at each other. Finally, VP spoke. "My friend" he said, "I have lived a long life and have known the bliss of True Enlightenment. You have your life ahead of you, you take a parachute, and I will go down with the plane."

MAGA smiled slowly and said "Hey, don't worry, VP. The world's smartest man just jumped out wearing my backpack."

*Trump and Pence landed safely and headed to the conference. At the conference, he met Braks Olama and asks him the difference between democrats and republicans as he never really understood what it was all about. So Olama made an analogy to help him understand.*

## 113. Two Cows

**DEMOCRAT**

You have two cows.
Your neighbor has none.
You feel guilty for being successful.
Lil Wayne sings about you.

**REPUBLICAN**

You have two cows.
Your neighbor has none.
So?

*At the conference Bracks Olama told them that the solution to the crisis was pumping more money into the economy (just like we did it in the state: quantitative easing) and withdrawing it later but the people did not understand and he had to use an analogy to help them to understand.*

## 114. Global crisis solution

Due to the economic crisis, a village that relied on tourism to survive had no tourists coming to the village. Everyone borrowed from everyone to survive. Months passed and the situation got worse. Then a tourist came along and booked a room. He paid for the room with a $100 dollars note. As soon as the tourist got to the room, the hotel owner ran to the butcher to pay his debt, the butcher took the money to the farmer whom he also owed money to and the farmer took the money to a prostitute whom he owed some rounds. The prostitute took the money to the hotel to pay her debt to the hotel owner as she was not able to pay when she took some rooms for her business. As she put down the money on the hotel owner's desk, the tourist came back from the room and told the owner that he was not satisfied with the room; he took his money back and left. Nothing spent, nothing won, and nothing lost.
Nevertheless no one in the village had debts now.

### 115. Who is trying to kiss May?

After the conference, MAGA, Macron and May were sitting in a train carriage together. The train went through a tunnel and there was complete darkness. Suddenly there was a kissing sound, then the sound of a really hard slap. When the train came out of the tunnel, MAGA and May were acting as if nothing had happened and Macron was holding the side of his face.

Macron was thinking MAGA must have tried to kiss May. She must have missed him and slapped me by mistake.

May thought to herself, Macron must have tried to kiss me but accidentally kissed MAGA and got slapped for it.

MAGA was thinking, brilliant, in the next tunnel; I will make

another kissing noise and slap the French twat again.

*MAGA wasn't voted in and lost his bid for a second presidential term; the new president made his life difficult, so he left the country.*

### 116. We can't complain

Trump applied for refugee status in South Africa. Because he was famous, a crowd of journalist was waiting for him at the airport. "So, Mr. Trump, what can you tell us about human rights in your country?"

"How man, right, oh, we cannot complain"

"Tell us about the political repression then?"

"Political repression? No, there also we cannot complain." "So why have you applied for political asylum in South Africa then?" "Well, because in South Africa you can complain."

*Before leaving his country, Trump's Chinese friend Fu gave him the address of his brother Hans Olaffsen who lives in South Africa and who had a shop in China town. He was wondering where Fu's brother got that name from so he went to visit him.*

## 117. Who changed my name?

Walking through Chinatown in South Africa, Trump was
fascinated with all the Chinese restaurants, shops, signs, and
banners. He turned a corner and saw a building with the sign "Hans
Olaffsen's Laundry." "Hans Olaffsen?" he mused. So he walked
into the shop and saw an old Chinese gentleman behind the
counter.

Trump asked:
"How did this place get a name like 'Hans Olaffsen's
Laundry?" The old man answered "Is name of owner."
Trump asked "Well, who and where is the
owner?" "Me... is right here" replied the old man.
"You, how did you ever get a name like Hans
Olaffsen?" "Is simple" said the old man.
"Many, many year ago when come to this country, was stand in line
at Documentation Centre. Man in front was big blonde Swede. Lady
look at him and say 'What your name?' She say 'Hans Olaffsen,'
then she look at me and go 'What your name?'"
"I say Sem Ting."

*Trump tries to sell nails and register his business, but the way
his new found journalist friend advertised the company quickly
put Trump out of business.*

## 118. With my nails, it's for eternity

Trump started his nail's company and told his friend about it.
He needed to do some advertising.
"Don't worry, I work for the Night Sun and I will try to
do something for you" said his friend
"Wonderful" said Trump
The next day, Trump bought the newspaper, he was horrified. He
saw Jesus on the cross and in small text it said 'With Trump's nails
it's for eternity.'
He called his friend and told him to quickly rectify the situation.
His friend agreed and told him not to worry.
The next day, Trump was anxious to see what his friend came up with.

He bought the paper and to his amazement he saw an empty cross with
Jesus' body lying next to the cross and the text read 'with

Trump's nails, it would have never happened.'

*Unable to get any financial help, Trump started to look for work opportunities and his rich neighbor was about to go on a holiday and left his dog under Trump's care, not knowing Trump was in a tight corner financially. This is what he needed.*

## 119. Why would I buy food for the dog while I am hungry?

J Pierraut who was living in South Africa, had a dog called Bobby, that he loved very much. He was about to go on a holiday to Paris and decided to leave his dog under the care of his neighbor, Trump. He gave Trump enough money to take care of the dog. Trump spent all the money and didn't have any left to take care of the dog, so the dog lost a lot of weight and Trump gained a lot of weight. When J. Pierraut returned and saw the state of his dog, he remarked with a lot of amazement and a surprised voice:

"Trump, the dog is so thin and you are so fat."

*As Trump became older, he returned to his country and was employed at a consulting firm. He began to develop some sleeping problems.*

## 120. Did the pill solve the problem or make it worse

Trump had this problem of getting up late in the morning and was always late for work. His boss was angry with him and threatened to fire him if he didn't do something about it.

So Trump went to his doctor who gave him a pill and told him to take it before he went to bed. Trump slept well, and in fact, beat the alarm in the morning. He had a leisurely breakfast and drove cheerfully to work.

"Boss" he said "The pill actually worked!"

"That's all fine" said the boss "But where were you yesterday?"

*Trump got onto a talk show and was boasting about some of his skills.*

## 121. I need to know that you are with me

Trump was interviewed by Oprah, and boasted that despite his seventy two years of age, he could still have sex three times a night. Stormy, who was also a guest, looked intrigued. After the show, Stormy said "Trump, if I am not being too forward, I'd love to have sex with an older man. Let's go back to my place."

So they went back to her place and had great sex. Afterwards, Trump said "If you think that was good, let me sleep for half an hour and we can have even better sex. But while I'm sleeping, hold my balls in your left hand and my penis in your right hand." Stormy looked a bit perplexed, but said "Okay". After half an hour he woke up and they had even better sex. Then Trump said "Stormy that was wonderful. But if you let me sleep for an hour, we can have the best sex yet. But again, hold my balls in your left hand and my penis in your right hand." Stormy was now used to the routine and complied. The results were mind blowing.

Once it was all over, and the cigarettes were lit, Stormy asked "Trump, tell me, does my holding your balls in my left hand and your penis in my right stimulate you while you're sleeping?"

Trump replied "No, but the last time I slept with a slut

from Louisiana, she stole my wallet."

*Trump continued to boast about his sexual endurance and unfortunately it got him fired.*

## 122. Three times a night or was it three nights?

The two old fellows, Trump and Pence were both only a year short of retirement. That didn't stop Trump from boasting to Pence about his sexual endurance. Trump boasted that he could have sex three times a night.

"Three times" gasped Pence admiringly "How do you do it?" "It was easy." Trump looked down modestly. "I made love to my wife, and then I rolled over and took a ten-minute nap. When I woke up again, I made love to her again and took another ten-minute nap. And then I put it to her again. Can you believe it! I woke up this morning feeling like a bull, I tell you."

"I got to try it" said Pence. "Hills won't believe its happening." So that night he made love to his wife, took a ten-minute nap, made love to her again, took another nap, woke up and made love to her a third time, then rolled over and fell sound asleep. He woke up feeling like a million bucks, pulled on his clothes, and ran to the office, where he found his boss waiting outside for him.

"What's up, Boss?" he asked. "I've been working for you for twenty years and never been late once. You aren't going to hold these twenty minutes against me now, are you?" "What twenty minutes?" growled the boss

"Where were you on Tuesday and Wednesday?"

*This is when Trump and Pence last worked and they were sent to their retirement home after this.*

# Chapter 4 x Melanie's school days

*Melanie was Trump's most present wife throughout his life, her childhood was normal so that's not worth Mentioning; her school days were another story. She was not always smart and she struggled a lot before finding her feet. Report time was a difficult time for her.*

### 123. School report

Melanie came back from school with her school report and it said that she had failed the year.

Her father was very angry and told her "you should be ashamed of yourself, failing like that, by the time he was your age, Putin was already in grade six."

Melanie replied "well, by the time he was your age he was already

the president."

*This incident inspired her to come out with tricky ways to present her parents with her report. Ways to dilute their anger and disappointment; here was one of the ways she used.*

### 124. The report was the least of her worries!!!

One day, at report time, Melanie's mom found a note on Melanie's bed, she immediately assumed the worst. In the note it was written:

*Dear mom,*

*I am writing to let you know that, unfortunately, I have left you to live with my boyfriend. Please don't look for me, we have run off to start a family in the forest. I am already pregnant, but don't worry, as I am already fourteen years old, I am technically an adult. My lack of experience will be compensated for by my boyfriend who is already forty four years of age. I really hope that science will discover a cure for AIDS for the sake of my boyfriend who is HIV positive. Well, I have to go now; we are catching a plane to Sri Lanka to visit my boyfriend's parents. I will return after two years to introduce you to your grandchildren. Hugs and kisses, Melanie.*

*PS: I am just joking, I am at the neighbor's, this is just to tell you, that there are more important things in life than a school report; you will find mine on the computer table. Love you mom.*

**After all these disappointment, her father decided to belittle her a bit in front of her peers.**

## 125. Are you coming in?

Melanie was going home after school. Suddenly, a car stopped alongside her, inside there was a single man.
- Hey, get in?
- No!
- Come on, I have sweets
- No
- Okay, if you get in, I will take you shopping - No
- Shit, what do you want from me then?
- Dad, I told you a thousand times not to fetch me in the Daewoo.

**While walking home after she refused to get in the car, Melanie came across a penguin in the street and decided to rescue it.**

## 126. A penguin in the street

Melanie found a penguin on the road; she picked it up and went to the police.
"I found a penguin. What do I do with it?"
"Well, I don't know. Take it to the zoo!"
The next day, the police saw her with the penguin.
"Didn't you take it to the zoo?
"Yes I did. He liked the zoo, so now we are going to the movies."

**Eventually she gave it up to the zoo. Her father was not happy with all she had been doing lately (school reports, penguins at home, refusing his lift). This incident may seem as if he implicitly was trying to hurt her.**

## 127. Assassination attempt

Melanie went to school with a big bandage around her head.
The teacher was worried.
"What happened to you?" asked the teacher
"A bee stung me" said Melanie
"Is this big bandage for one small sting?" asked the teacher
Melanie replied "Dad killed it with a shovel."

*After the shovel incident, Melanie's school marks mysteriously improved and that gave her the confidence to pursue her studies until she graduated.*

*Just before graduation, the students decided to bring their teachers gifts as a sign of appreciation.*

## 128. Guess what I got you?

The florist's son handed her a gift. She shook it, held it overhead, and said "I bet I know what it is. Some flowers." "That's right" the boy said "but how did you know?" "Oh, just a wild guess" she said. The next pupil was the candy shop owner's daughter. The teacher held her gift overhead, shook it, and said "I bet I can guess what it is: A box of sweets." "That's right, but how did you know?" asked the girl. "Oh, just a wild guess" said the teacher.
The next gift was from Melanie and her father was running the biggest liquor franchise stores in the country. The teacher held the package overhead and it was leaking. She touched a drop of the leakage with her finger and touched it to her tongue. "Is it wine?" she asked. "No" Melanie replied, with some excitement. The teacher took one more taste before declaring "I give up. What is it?" With great glee, Melanie replied: "It's a puppy!"

*After Melanie had graduated, she became interested in cooking.*

## 129. Why is this cookbook so fancy?

Melanie and her best friend were talking after their graduation, their conversation drifted from politics to cooking. "I got a cookbook once" said Melanie, "but I could never do anything with it." "Too much fancy work in it, eh?" asked her best friend. "You said it" said

Melanie, "every one of the recipes begins the same way "Take a clean dish."

# Chapter 5 x Melanie's career

*Melanie kicked off her working career in the family firm and she quickly reached the top.*

### 130. The promotion
The boss called one of his employees into his office.
"Well you have been with us for a year now, you have started as a receptionist, after a week you became an advertising manager, after a month you were promoted to head of HR, four months later you became the vice-president of the company and now I am about to retire and I would like to nominate you as the president of the company. Congratulations!
"Thanks."
"Is that all you have to say???" asked the boss.
"Thanks Daddy."

*Melanie eventually bankrupted the family company and had to look for another job, so she sent out her CV and was invited to write a test and see if she would get hired.*

### 131. Job Interview
Melanie and another woman had applied for the same job. As they had the same qualification, the head of HR made them answer a quiz in order to select the appropriate candidate. The two answered nine of the ten questions. The Head of HR called Melanie in and explained: "You both got the same result but I have hired the other candidate." Disappointed, Melanie asked why the other woman was chosen considering they got the same result.
"I have not based my decision on the correct answer but I have based

my decision on the wrong answer."

Puzzled, Melanie asked how a wrong answer can be more wrong than another.

The Manager said it was simple "on question number seven the other women wrote, she doesn't know and you wrote me neither."

*Below is one of the tests that Melanie was given.*

## 132. Humor as a professional test

The following short quiz consisted of four questions and told whether you were qualified to be a "professional." Scroll down for the answers after you have thought about the answer.

1. How do you put a giraffe into a refrigerator?

The correct answer is: Open the refrigerator; put in the giraffe and close the door. This question tests whether you tend to do simple things in an overly complicated way.

2. How do you put an elephant into a refrigerator?

Wrong Answer: Open the refrigerator; put in the elephant and close the refrigerator.

Correct Answer: Open the refrigerator, take out the giraffe, put in the elephant and close the door. This tests your ability to think through the repercussions of your actions.

3. The Lion King is hosting an animal conference; all the animals attend, except one. Which animal does not attend?

Correct Answer: The Elephant. The Elephant is in the refrigerator. This tests your memory.

OK, even if you did not answer the first three questions correctly, you still have one more chance to show your abilities.

4. There is a river you must cross. But it is inhabited by crocodiles. How do you manage it?

Correct Answer: You swim across. All the crocodiles are attending the animal meeting. This tests whether you learn quickly from your mistakes.

*As she failed the test, she was given the option to rewrite the test or go for a class with a number of other ladies who had failed the test as well.*

## 133. Who discovered America?

The teacher was giving a history lesson to twenty
ladies. First question: Where is America on the map?
Melanie stood up and found America on the
map. Second question: Who discovered
America? The nineteen remaining ladies stood
up and said, "Melanie did."

*After the short course, they were given another test.*

## 134. Brain Exercise

"Exercise of the brain is as important as exercise of the muscles.
As we grow older, it's important that we keep mentally alert.
The saying: 'If you don't use it, you will lose it' also applies to
the brain."

"Below is a very private way to gauge your loss or non-loss of
intelligence. So take the following test presented here and determine
if you are losing it or are still a MENSA candidate. OK, relax, clear
your mind and . . . Begin" said the invigilator.

1. What do you put in a toaster?
The answer is bread. If you said "toast" then give up now and go do
something else and try not to hurt yourself. If you said "bread", go
to question 2.

2. Say "silk" five times. Now spell "silk". What do cows drink?
Answer: Cows drink water. If you said "milk", please do not attempt
the next question. Your brain is obviously overstressed and may
even overheat. It may be that you need to content yourself with
reading something more appropriate such as "Children's World". If
you said "water" then proceed to question three.

3. If a red house is made from red bricks and a blue house is made
from blue bricks and a pink house is made from pink bricks and a
black house is made from black bricks, what is a greenhouse made
from?
Answer: Greenhouses are made from glass. If you said "green
bricks", what the heck are you still doing here reading these
questions? If you said "glass", then go on to question four.

4. Thirty years ago, a plane was flying at twenty thousand feet over

Germany. If you will recall, Germany at that time was politically divided into West Germany and East Germany. Anyway, during the flight, TWO of the engines fail. The pilot, realizing that the last remaining engine was also failing, decided on a crash landing procedure. Unfortunately the engine failed before he had time to do this and the plane crashed, smack in the middle of "no man's land" between East Germany and West Germany. Where would you bury the survivors? East Germany, West Germany or in no man's land? Answer: You don't, of course, bury survivors. If you said ANYTHING else, you are a real dunce and you must NEVER try to rescue anyone from a plane crash. Your efforts would not be appreciated. If you said, "You don't bury the survivors" then proceed to the next question.

5. If the hour hand on a clock moves 1/60th of a degree every minute then how many degrees will the hour hand move in one hour? Answer: One degree. If you said "360 degrees" or anything other than "one degree", you are to be congratulated on getting this far, but you are obviously out of your league. Turn your pencil in and exit the room. Everyone else proceed to the final question.

6. without using a calculator. You are driving a bus from London to Paris. In London, seventeen people get on the bus. In Readorg, six people get off the bus and nine people get on. In Swindon, two people get off and four get on. In Cardiff, eleven people get off and sixteen people get on. In Swansea, three people get off and five people get on. In Carmathen, six people get off and three get on. You then arrive at Milford Haven. What was the name of the bus driver?

Answer: Oh, for goodness sake! It was YOU, Read the first line!!!

*Fortunately after writing the test for a second time, she finally got the job as a receptionist and he had trouble understanding what some of the French guests really wanted.*

### 135. Toilette Pepper please

A French guest, who was staying in her hotel, realized that he had run out of toilet paper and called room service for some "pepper". "Black pepper or white pepper?" asked Melanie. "Toilet pepper!" responded the guest

*A Swiss man checked in and it seemed that he was very thirsty.*

## 136. Give me a Glass of water, my room is on fire

The Swiss man went down from his hotel room to the reception. He woke Melanie who was already sleeping and asked for a glass of water. Melanie gave him the glass of water and went back to sleep. Fifteen minutes later, the same client returned and asked for another glass of water. Melanie gave it to him and rushed back to sleep. He returned a few more times after that, until eventually Melanie became irritated.

"What have you eaten to be this thirsty" she asked.

"I am not thirsty, there is fire in my room" he replied.

*Fire fighters were called but it was too late and the hotel burned to the ground. So Melanie had to look for another job. She decided to move to another country as there might be more opportunities there. On her way there, she met a lawyer.*

## 137. Is it worth $5 or $100?

The lawyer and Melanie were sitting next to each other on the plane, it was a long flight.

The lawyer asked Melanie if she would like to play an entertaining game. Melanie was tired and declined the offer but the lawyer insisted and explained that the game was very simple. "I ask you a question and if you don't know the answer, you give me five dollars and vice versa."

Again Melanie politely declined the offer but the lawyer insisted. "Okay, lets say if I ask you a question and you don't know the answer, you give me five dollars and if you ask me a question that I don't know, I will give you one hundred dollars."

That got Melanie interested and she finally accepted to play the game. The lawyer began "What is the distance between the earth and moon?"

Melanie could not answer, so she gave five dollars to the lawyer. "Your turn!" said the lawyer.

Melanie asked "What goes up the hill with three feet and comes back with four?"

The lawyer thought for a very long time and decided that he didn't know the answer so he handed one hundred dollars to Melanie.

"What is the answer?" he asked Melanie

Melanie opened up her purse and gave him another five dollars.

*Unfortunately, the plane crashed in the ocean and eleven people survived and were rescued by a helicopter. They were being taken to the airport.*

## 138. We need someone off this rope

The plane crashed in the ocean and eleven people survived and were rescued by a helicopter. They were hanging on a rope under the helicopter. There were ten men and Melanie was the only woman. The rope was not strong enough to carry them all, so they decided that one had to drop off, otherwise they were all going to fall. They were having trouble deciding who that person would be, but then Melanie made a very touching speech. She said that she would voluntarily let go of the rope, because as a woman she was used to giving up everything for her husband and kids, and for men in general, without ever getting anything in return.

As soon as she finished her speech, all the men started clapping their hands.

*After the incident, she was safely brought to the airport with some of her possessions. While she waited at customs, she sat next to a priest*

## 139. At the airport

She asked him "Father, can I ask you for a favor?"

"Of course my child what can I do for you?"

"I bought a very sophisticated electric hair dryer for my mom's birthday. It's still in its original packaging and its value is well beyond the maximum allowed to import; so I am worried it might be confiscated. Can't you take it through the customs for me, under your cassock for instance?"

"I would like to help you my child, but I am warning you that I will never lie."

"With the honesty reflecting from your face, they won't bother to question you" said Melanie.

When they got to customs, Melanie let the priest go first and the custom officer asked:

"Do you have something to declare father?"

"From the tips of my hair to my hips, I don't have something to declare."

The custom officer found this answer slightly strange and asked: "What about from your hips to your toes, do you have something to declare?"

"I have a tool that is about to be manipulated by a woman, the tool has not been used before."

Hearing this answer, the custom officer laughed and let him

go through.

*The kindness of the priest combined with the accident that she had just survived motivated her to join the monastery and become a nun. After joining, the monastery went to a charity event.*

## 140. Show this Dracula your true colors sister

Melanie and another nun drove through the forest by car. They were feeling slightly nervous. When they stopped on the side of the road to rest, they were startled when suddenly, out of nowhere, a diminutive Dracula jumped onto the hood of the car and hissed through the windshield.

"Quick, quick!" shouted the other Sister. "Turn the wipers on! That will get rid of the abomination!" Sister Melanie switched them on, knocking Dracula about, but he clung on and continues hissing at the nuns.

"What now?" "Switch on the windshield washer! I filled it up with Holy Water before we left" said the Sister. Dracula screamed as the water burned his skin, but he clung on and continued hissing at the nuns.

"My goodness, now what shall we do?" said worried Sister Melanie.

"Show him your cross" said the other Sister.

"Now you're talking" said Sister Melanie as she rolled down the

window, she leaned out and screamed, "Get the fuck off our

car!"

*The Monastery was going through some financial difficulties and needed to raise money, so the sisters were put in charge of selling cupcakes.*

## 141. The Sister's logic

Sister Melanie and Sister Pallin went to sell cupcakes.

Sister Melanie: It's late and we are very far from the monastery.

Sister Pallin: Did you notice that a guy has been following us for more than an hour?

Sister Melanie: Yes, what do you think he wants?

Sister Pallin: It's obvious, he wants to rape us.

Sister Melanie: So what do we do now? He is going to get us in less than a minute.

Sister Pallin: The only logical thing to do is to separate. You go right and I will go left. He can't follow both of us.

At that point the man decided to follow Sister Pallin.

**Sister Melanie arrived at the monastery first and was worried about** Sister Pallin.

After a while Sister Pallin arrived.

Sister Melanie: Sister Pallin, thank God you are here! Tell me what happened?

Sister Pallin: well isn't it obvious! The man couldn't follow us both and decided to follow me instead.

Sister Melanie: "So what happened?"

Sister Pallin: Well, isn't it obvious! I started running as fast as I could and he did the same

Sister Melanie: And then?

Sister Pallin: Well isn't it obvious! He caught me.

Sister Melanie: Oh my God, what did you do?

Sister Pallin: Well, isn't it obvious? I lifted my dress.

Sister Melanie: Oh Sister Marla, what did he do?

Sister Pallin: Well, isn't it obvious? He took down his pants.

Sister Melanie: Oh God, what happened then?

Sister Pallin: Once again, isn't it obvious sister? A sister with a dress up runs faster than a man with his pants down.

PS: If you were thinking of another ending, you might have to

check your mind for some pervert tendencies.

> *Melanie and the head Priest were on their way to visit a poor church up in the mountain and they got lost.*

## 142. Sister let's pretend we were married for the night

They were trapped in the mountain and there was a storm. After a while, they found a small hut. Tired, they decide to sleep in there until the weather cleared. There was a pile of sheets and a duvet on the floor, but only one bed.

The Priest, who was a gentleman said "Sister, you will sleep on the bed and I will sleep on the floor, under the duvet".

As he lay on the duvet, Melanie said "Father, I am feeling cold."

He got up and placed the sheet from the pile on top of her. He crawled back into his duvet and had just closed his eyes when again Melanie called "Father, I am still feeling cold."

The priest got up again and placed another sheet on top of her. He crawled back into his duvet and fell asleep. She woke him again, to complain. The priest said:

"My child, I have an idea, we are here in the middle of nowhere and no one will ever find out what is about to happen. Let's act as if we were married"

Exhausted Melanie agreed "OK father, let's do that, "she said

suddenly the Father shouted out "Get off your ass and go get the

fucking sheet yourself bitch!!!

*After the trip, Melanie no longer wanted to be a Nun and decided to leave the monastery and become a journalist.*

## 143. Mad cow disease

Melanie was an ambitious journalist and wanted to investigate the origin of the mad cow disease. She went very deep into farm areas, where apparently, one old farmer thought he had discovered the origin of the disease.

- Good morning sir

- Good morning ma'am

- It is rumored that you know why cows seem to get this terrible disease?

- Yes, you probably know that the bull is presented to the cow once a year.

- Yes, but I don't see what that has to do with the disease.

- You also probably know the cows are milked twice a

day? - Yes, but I still don't see the link with the disease.

- Well, if your breasts where groped twice a day and you only had sex once a year, wouldn't you go crazy???

*Melanie went to Jerusalem for her next story.*

## 144. How is the prayer going?

In Jerusalem, Melanie heard about an old Rabbi who visited the Wailing Wall to pray, twice a day, every day, for a long, long time. In an effort to verify the story, she went to the site and there he was! She watched the bearded old man at prayer and after about forty five minutes, when he turned to leave, she approached him for an interview.

"I'm Melanie from Triple N Sir, how long have you been coming to the Wailing Wall and praying?" For about fifty years, he informed her. Fifty years! "That's amazing! What do you pray for?" "I pray for peace between the Jews and the Arabs. I pray for all the hatred to stop and I pray for all our children to grow up in safety and friendship." "And how do you feel, Sir, after doing this for fifty years?"

"Like I'm talking to a wall"

*Melanie joined the police force and had to pass a test.*

## 145. Can I join the police?

The police were in the process of recruiting. Melanie and two other women were being tested that day. Today they were testing their physiognomic skills. He showed them a picture of a person for five seconds and then hid it away. He told them that this was a suspect. They had to describe the person in the picture. The first women said "It's easy; we will catch him quickly because he only has one eye." The police man replied, "This is a profile picture and you can only see one eye."

He asked the second women to describe the person. She replied "It's easy, he only has one ear."

The police man got angry and started to lose all hope on these candidates.

He asked Melanie the same question and added "think carefully before talking shit."

Melanie thought for a minute and then said "it's easy, he is wearing contact lenses."

The policeman couldn't believe his ears and he went to check this fact, to his amazement the fact was true. He came back and asked Melanie how she knew he had contact lenses. Melanie replied "It's easy; he can't wear glasses if he only has one ear and one eye."

*Melanie was finally accepted into the police force. She stopped a lady for speeding.*

## 146. I didn't realize that you are a police officer

A lady was speeding down the highway with her sports car.
Melanie stopped her and asked:
"Drivers license please."
Panicked the lady searched through her bag and asked "What does it look like?"
"Rectangular with your picture on" replied Melanie
The lady continued her search and found a mirror; she looked inside it and handed it to Melanie.
Melanie opened the mirror, looked inside and said:
"That's okay, you can go, I didn't realize that you were also from

the police!"

*Melanie tried to double her income by doing prostitution on the side but she quickly changed her mind.*

## 147. I am a new prostitute

In a bar, Melanie sat next to a guy and whispered in his ear:
"For $500, you will have a good time with me, I guarantee it."
"What about $1000?" asked the guy
"Wonderful, what would you want me to do for that amount?" "Nothing much, you will just have to let me beat you a bit." "And what do you call a bit."
"Well, until you give me back my money."

*She left prostitution and looked for a job in a factory but she didn't understand what she had to do.*

## 148. Tickle Me Elmo

There was a factory in the North Pole which made the Tickle Me Elmo toys. The toy laughed when you tickled it under the arms. Melanie got a job at The Tickle Me Elmo factory and she reported for her first day promptly at 8:00 am.

The next day at 8:45 am there was a knock at the Personnel Manager's door. The Foreman threw open the door and began to complain about the new employee. He complained that she was incredibly slow and the whole line was backing up, putting the entire production line behind schedule.

The Personnel Manager decided he should see this for himself, so the two men marched down to the factory floor. When they get there the line was so backed up that there were Tickle Me Elmo's all over the factory floor and they were really beginning to pile up. At the end of the line stood Melanie surrounded by mountains of Tickle Me Elmo's.

She had a roll of plush red fabric and a huge bag of small marbles. The two men watched in amazement as she cut little pieces of fabric, wrapped it around two marbles and began to carefully sew the little package between Elmo's legs.

The Personnel Manager burst into laughter. After several minutes of hysterics he pulled himself together and approached Melanie. "I'm sorry" he said to her, barely able to keep a straight face "but I think you misunderstood the instructions I gave you yesterday."

"Your job is to give Elmo two test tickles."

*Melanie soon got bored dealing with all those Tickle Me Elmo's, so she started working at a filling station where she could deal directly with people.*

## 149. Fill up the tank of the UFO with UF only

A flying saucer landed at the station where Melanie is now working. The two space aliens inside seemed completely unconcerned about being detected, in fact, the letters "UFO" were emblazoned in big, bold letters on one side of their shiny craft. As the station owner stood and gawked in silence, paralyzed with shock, Melanie nonchalantly filled up the tank and waved to the two aliens as they took off.

"Do you realize what just happened?" The station owner finally uttered.

"Yeah" said Melanie. "So?"

"Didn't you see the space aliens in that vehicle?!"

"Yeah" repeated Melanie. "So?"

"Didn't you see the letters 'UFO' on the side of that vehicle?!" "Yeah" repeated Melanie. "So?"

"Don't you know what 'UFO' means?!"

Melanie rolled her eyes. "Good grief, boss! I've been working here for a week; Of course I know what 'UFO' means

"Unleaded Fuel Only"

*Melanie was also an accomplished carpenter and did some carpentry from time to time.*

## 150. The nail is defective if it's pointing at you

Melanie and her co-worker were working on a house. Melanie who was nailing down siding would reach into her nail pouch, pull out a nail and either toss it over her shoulder or nail it in.

The co-worker, figuring this was worth looking into, asked "Why are you throwing those nails away?"

Melanie explained "If I pull a nail out of my pouch and it's pointing toward me, I throw it away because it's defective. If it's pointing toward the house, then I nail it in!"

The co-worker got completely upset and yelled "You moron! The nails pointing toward you aren't defective! They're for the other side of the house!"

*After she had completed her work, she was asked to change light bulb.*

## 151. We need help changing a light bulb

Melanie and her co-workers were struggling to change the light bulb.

Melanie decided to call 911.

Melanie: We need help. We are three carpenters trying to change a light bulb.

Operator: Hmmmmm, You put in a fresh bulb?

Melanie: Yes.

Operator: The power in the house is on?

80

Melanie: Of course.

Operator: And the switch is on?

Melanie: Yes, yes.

Operator: And the bulb still won't light up?

Melanie: No, it's working fine.

Operator: Then what's the problem?

Melanie: We got dizzy spinning the ladder around, and we all fell

and hurt ourselves.

*After they recovered and were discharged from hospital, they took on a job that involved a talking mirror.*

## 152. I think I am thinking

Melanie and her two co-workers were standing in front of a mirror. The mirror suddenly spoke and asked them to reveal their thoughts. It said if their thoughts were true, they would get $1000000, but if their thoughts were false, they would get sucked into the mirror. The first friend: I think my second friend is cleverer than I.

Poof! And she disappears into the mirror.

The second friend: I think my first friend was the most beautiful.

Poof! She also disappears into the mirror.

Melanie: "I think ...

Poof! She also disappears into the mirror.

# Chapter 6 x Melanie's dating background

*Melanie has had her share of dating with many different experiences. It wasn't always smooth and easy. She had to go through some plastic surgery and transformation in order to get her first date.*

### 153. You must be single

As Melanie walked into a store, she bought the following:

1 small box of detergent

1 bar of soap

3 individual servings of yoghurt

2 oranges

She then went to the cashier.

Cashier: Oh, you must be single

Melanie: You can tell that by what I bought?

Cashier: No, you're very ugly!

*She had plastic surgery, which gave her the face of an angel. Her friend immediately set her up on a blind date to meet this new guy.*

### 154. Your Grandpa needs to die or mine will

Halfway through the date, after being with Melanie all evening, the boy was bored and couldn't take another minute of this blind date. Earlier, he had secretly arranged to have a friend call him on the phone so he would have an excuse to leave if something like this happened.

The phone rang and he left the table to take the call. When he returned to the table, he lowered his eyes, put on a grim expression and said "I have some bad news. My Grandpa just died."

"Thank heavens" Melanie replied. "If yours hadn't, mine would have

had to!"

*Melanie decided that blind dates weren't for her and started going out to parties, and she met another interesting guy named Tits....*

### 155. My name is Car-men, because that is what I like.

Melanie arrived at a party. While scanning the guests, she spotted an attractive man standing alone. She approached him, smiled and said "Hello. My name is Carmen." "That's a beautiful name" he replied. "Is it a family name?" "No" she replied. As a matter of fact I gave it to myself. It represents the things that I enjoy the most: cars and men. Therefore I chose "Carmen". "What's your name?" She asked. He answered "B.J. Titsengolf."

*She got on well with that guy and they started going out. After months of dating he wanted to get physically intimate, but she was too young. They decided that when she was finally of legal age, she was going to lose her virginity in his car. So on the night after they had been to the movies, they found an isolated spot and waited for the moment the clock reached that time.*

### 156. She will be sixteen in twelve minutes

A policeman was patrolling a local parking lot, overlooking a golf course. He drove by a car and saw a couple inside with the dome light on. There was a young man in the driver's seat reading a computer magazine and a young lady in the back seat knitting. He stopped to investigate. He walked up to the driver's window and knocked. The young man looked up, cranked the window down, and said "Yes Officer?"

"What are you doing?" the policeman asked. "What does it look like?" answered the young man. "I'm reading this magazine."

Pointing towards Melanie in the back seat, the officer then asked "And what is she doing?" The young man looked over his shoulder and replied "What does it look like? She's knitting."

"And how old are you?" the officer then asked the young man. "I'm nineteen" he replied. "And how old is she?" asked the officer.

The young man looked at his watch and said "Well, in about twelve minutes she'll be sixteen."

*The policeman being a conservative father decided that he was not going to allow that to happen and as the boy did not have a license, he encouraged him into driving the young girl home, under his escort. Their hope of some action vanished. Broken hearted and disappointed, he reluctantly took Melanie home and avoided getting into trouble with the policeman.*

*The young man and Melanie decided they were going for another proper date and before leaving for the date, Grandma called her to give her some advice about boys.*

## 157. Don't let him disgrace our family

Her grandmother said "Sit here and let me tell you about those young boys. He is going to try and kiss you, you are going to like that, but don't let him do that. He is going to try and feel your breasts, you are going to like that, but don't let him do that. But most important, he is going to try and get on top of you to have his way with you. You are going to like that, but don't let him do that. It will disgrace the family."

With that bit of advice, Melanie went on her date. The next day she told Grandma that her date went just like she had predicted. Grandma, I didn't let him disgrace the family. When he tried, I just turned over, got on top of him, and disgraced HIS family"

*Granny fainted and when she woke up, she decided that the family was indeed disgraced and forced Melanie to move out as she had become a woman now. The relationship with her family was difficult during that time but eventually they made peace and her Grandma finally agreed to visit her in her new flat which she shared with a male roommate, named Young.*

## 158. Mom, did you steal the silver spoon?

Melanie invited her grandmother to dinner. During the meal, she noticed that Young was very handsome. She observed the way they behaved with each other and she wondered if there was anything going on between them beyond sharing the apartment. Melanie guessed her grandmothers thoughts and said:

"Grandma, I know what you are thinking but I can assure you that Young and I are only sharing this apartment and nothing else." A week later, Young says to Melanie "Since your grandma left, I can't find our silver spoon?"

"I will be surprised if grandma has become a pickpocket! I will send her an e-mail to clarify the situation."

In the e-mail she wrote:

*Dear Grandma*
*I am not saying you took our silver spoon and I am also not saying You didn't take it but the fact is since you left, it seems like the silver spoon has disappeared*
*Love from Melanie'*

The next day, Melanie received an e-mail from her grandmother. *Dear Melanie*

*I am not saying you are sleeping with Young, I am also not saying you are not sleeping with him but the fact is, if Young was sleeping in his own room, he would have found the silver spoon a long time ago. Love from your Grandma*

# Chapter 7 x Trump's married life

*Trump met the "girl of his dreams," Melanie. He immediately fell in love with her. He invited her to dinner. That night he went to fetch her.*

### 159. I need to fart discreetly

Melanie was very nervous about her first date with Trump. She'd been attracted to him for a long time. When he came to her door, her stomach started to turn and she realized the chili she had eaten for lunch had been a bad idea. Trump opened the door for her and as he walked around to his side, she farted loudly and quickly opened the window hoping he would not notice. She was horrified when Trump gestured to the back seat and said: "Have you met Pence and Pen?"

*They went to Trump's usual restaurant because it was the only restaurant around. Trump was not usually impressed with the quality of their service.*

### 160. What did you serve me yesterday?

Trump ordered from the menu "I'd like one under-cooked egg so that it's runny, and one over-cooked egg so that it's tough and hard to eat. I'd also like grilled bacon which is a bit on the cold side, burnt toast, butter straight from the freezer so that it's impossible to spread and a pot of very weak, lukewarm coffee." "That's a complicated order sir" said the bewildered waiter. "It might be quite difficult." Trump replied sarcastically "but it can't be that difficult because that's exactly what you brought me yesterday!"

### 161. SMS love

Melanie sent Trump the following text:

My love,

If you are sleeping, send me your dreams.

If you are laughing, send me your smiles.

If you are crying, send me your tears.

I love you.

Trump replied:

I am taking a dump,

I am sending you something though.

*The following night they went to the same restaurant again and Trump proposed to Melanie. She was a bit hesitant though.*

### 162. Marry him to make him believe in hell

Melanie came home from a date with Trump and rather sadly she said to her mother:

"Trump proposed to me an hour ago."

"Then why are you so sad?" her mother asked.

"Because he also told me he is an atheist."

Mom, he doesn't even believe there is a Hell."

Her mother replied "Marry him anyway. Between the two of

us, we'll show him just how wrong he is."

*Eventually she accepted Trump's proposal, but Trump still had to convince her parents that he was good enough for their daughter. There were two other suitors, Trump had to compete with.*

### 163. Eat that spice and you will marry my daughter

Melanie's father would only offer her hand in marriage to whoever could eat the most "tchipa spice" (the hottest spice) without complaint; because he didn't want any complaints after the marriage. The first suitor hoping to marry Melanie arrived and as soon as he started to eat the chilly, he started to sneeze and sniff.

The second suitor began eating the tchipa; he too began to sneeze and sniff. Then it was Trump's turn. As soon as he began eating the chili, he disguised his sneezing and sniffing by speaking at the same time. "The first guy was sniffing like this and sneezing like atchim but me I usually sniff like "sniff sniff", but as I am used to this Tchipa, I won't do all that. The second guy was sniffing like this and sneezing like atshooo, but me, I usually sneeze like achooom, but I won't complain because I'm used to this Tchipa, not like those other guys"

*Trump was happy to have passed the first test but he still had one more test to pass in order to win Melanie's hand in marriage.*

## 164. Always keep condoms in the car

Trump and Melanie had been going out for more than a year, before they decided to get married, although there was one thing that concerned Trump. It was Melanie's little sister, she was twenty two years old and always wore tight T-shirts most of the time with no bra and every time she bend down, Trump was overcome with a wonderful feeling that bothered him. She also only seemed to do this in front of Trump.

One day, Melanie's little sister invited Trump over to show him the wedding invitations cards. When he got there, she said she was lonely and had feelings for him. She told him she only needed him once before he married her sister. He was speechless and incapable of saying anything.

She said "I am going to my room and if you are ready for the adventure, join me."

Trump stood paralyzed with disbelief as he watched her go upstairs. He then dashed outside to his car. Melanie's entire family was waiting there, they applauded him and his father in law's eyes filled with tears. He hugged him and welcomed him into the family, saying that he couldn't have hoped for a better son in law.

Moral of the story: Always keep your condoms in your car.

*So Trump passed the first test with tricks and condoms had saved him in the second. So now he had the green light to marry Melanie. Although he had one more thing he needed to fix.*

## 165. This frog hates me

Trump had a 12inch long penis. It was more of an inconvenience than a blessing. He looked everywhere for a solution within the medical field to shorten his penis. Unfortunately no one could help him. He then went to all types of healers, but they could not help him. Finally he heard of an old man living in the bush who might be able to help him. He immediately went to see him.

The old man said "you got the wrong information; I do the opposite of what you need. If you give me some money, I can give you the address of a frog that does what you need; if you ask him a question and he says no, your engine's size will get 2 inches shorter and if he says yes, the opposite will happen. Trump agreed and gave the old man some money. He went to the frog and asked "Little frog will you marry me?"

"No!" said the frog.

Trump's penis shortened 2 inches.

Again he asked "little frog, will you marry me?"

"No!" repeated the frog.

Again Trump's penis shortened 2 inches.

He thought to himself "wow! Girls, here I come. One more time and it will be the right size."

"Little frog will you marry me?"

"NO, no, no, no, no, and no" said the frog

*Fortunately for him the old man he initially met helped him get some of his size back and he now had the size that he always wanted.*


*Meanwhile Melanie was also getting ready for her wedding; she went with her grandpa and her friend to buy her wedding dress. She broke the news to her friend on their way.*


## 166. Don't marry him, he is a liar

Melanie and her best friend were talking. Melanie said:
"You know what? I'm getting married and you know he can't stop telling me how pretty I am."
Her friend replied by saying "It's not a good idea to marry someone who starts off a relationship by lying to you."

## 167. You can pay me with kisses

She walked up to the counter and said "I would like to buy this fabric for my wedding dress. How much does it cost?" "Only one kiss per yard" replied the male clerk with a smirk. "That's fine" said Melanie. "I'll take ten yards." With expectation and anticipation written all over his face, the clerk quickly measured out the cloth, wrapped it up then teasingly held it out.
Melanie snapped up the package, pointed to the old man

standing beside her and smiled "Grandpa will pay the bill."

*When Melanie walked out of the shop, she saw a queue of people waiting to see a Wise man. She thought she would ask him for some advice as well, so she took her place in the queue. While waiting, she heard what the other people discussed with the Wise man.*

## 168. The Wise man does not agree

One man said to the Wise man "The ground is on our heads today." The wise man stood quietly, as a sign that he agreed.
Another man said to the Wise man "The sky is under our feet today."
The Wise man stood quietly as a sign that he agreed.
A third man said to the Wise man
"I saw four women sitting in one place for an entire hour and none of them uttered a word."
The wise finally spoke and said:
"NO, that's impossible."

*Melanie finally got a chance to ask the wise man her question.*

## 169. The magical key

Melanie asked the wise man, why is it that when men have many girlfriends at the same time, they are considered as 'cool', but when women have many boyfriends at one time, they are thought of as 'sluts'.
The Wise man replied "It is only normal to consider a key that can

90

open many locks as magical while a lock which can be opened by any key is considered useless."

*It was finally the day of the wedding and Trump was on his way to get married. Unfortunately he was stopped by a traffic officer because he was speeding and he didn't have his license. He tried telling the traffic officer that this was his wedding day, but he wouldn't let him speak.*

## 170. The Groom was in jail while the people were waiting
"But, officer" Trump began "I can explain."
"Just be quiet" snapped the officer. "I'm going to let you cool your heels in jail until the Chief gets back." "But, officer, I just wanted to say..."
"I said keep quiet! You're going to jail!"
A few hours later the officer checked on his prisoner and said: "Lucky for you that it's the Chief's niece's wedding so he will be in a good mood when he gets back."
"Don't count on it" answered Trump "I'm the groom."

*Fortunately the traffic officer feared the wrath of the Chief; so with great haste he personally escorted Trump to his wedding. Trump managed to get there before the guests started leaving.*

*The wedding was over; Trump and his wife were off to their honeymoon to a hotel in the South.*

## 171. Lets act as if we are an old couple
Melanie felt slightly embarrassed to be thought of as a honeymooner; so when they arrived at their hotel, she asked him if there was any way that they could make it appear that they had been married for a long time. He responded "Sure. You carry the suitcases!"

*While on honeymoon Trump tried to show off to his new bride but she soon put him in his place.*

## 172. How much is that love?
They were arguing about what they should do that day. Trying to assert himself, Trump exploded "If it weren't for my money, we wouldn't be here at all!"

Melanie replied "You are right my dear, if it weren't for your lovely fortune, we wouldn't be in the South, we wouldn't be on a honeymoon and there wouldn't even be any 'we' in the first place."

*They were in their honeymoon suite and there was a problem that Melanie was trying to solve.*

## 173. One is definitely nicer than two

After their wedding it became clear that Trump didn't know anything about marriage. He thought that marriage was all about the woman cooking and cleaning as he never knew or heard anything about sex. Melanie was not happy about this. Melanie went to see Trump's doctor and complained about the situation.

Melanie made an appointment for herself and Trump to see the doctor. When they got there, the doctor asked Trump and Melanie to take off their clothes. He showed Trump a part of his body and a private place on his wife's body and said, when I say 'one' you put this thing there, when I say two, you take it out, Okay."

Let's go, one, it's in, two it's out. One, two, one two, one, two. Trump started to enjoy this exercise and said to the doctor.

"Doctor, one is nicer than two."

The doctor replied "Okay, but if you don't do two how you going to do one?"

*The problem was solved; Trump and Melanie were off to the golf course.*

## 174. How old is your husband

They were playing golf in a very expensive neighborhood, surrounded by very beautiful and expensive houses. At the third hole, Trump said to his wife:

"Baby, be careful not to hit the ball through the window of one of these houses, it will cost us a fortune to fix."

Just then Melanie hit the ball and the ball went straight through the biggest glass window in the most beautiful house. Trump was very angry and they went to knock on the door of the house to investigate. A man answered.

"Come in" he said.

They went in and saw the glass all over the floor as well as a broken bottle in the corner. The man then said:

"Are you the ones who broke the glass?" "Yes, but we are very sorry."

"No need, the truth is that I am a Genie and was a prisoner in that bottle for one thousand years, so the two of you, by accident, freed me. To thank you, I would like to make three of your wishes come true. As there are two of you, I will give each one a wish and keep the third one for myself. What would you like to wish for?"

"I would like to earn a million dollars a month" said Trump

"Consider it done, from tomorrow you will start earning that. What about you?" He asked Melanie.

"I would like to have a house in every city of the world?"

"Of course" said the Genie. Tomorrow you will get the title deeds of all your properties.

"What about you" said Trump to the Genie, what would you like?

"I have been locked in this bottle for one thousand years and I have not had sex for all that time, so I would like to have sex with your wife."

Trump thought about it and decided that a million dollars a month was worth it, so he would make an exception this time. He asked Melanie if this was alright with her.

"No problem" she said.

The Genie took Melanie upstairs and they have sex for two hours, when they were done, the Genie asked Melanie:

"How old is your husband?"

"Forty years old. Why?"

"Because it's unbelievable that people of that age still believe in Genies."

*This incident caused Trump to lose all trust in Genies, except for Djinna. He wanted to leave the hotel immediately and go home but he still had to pay for the bill.*

## 175. Touch it or not, you will pay for it

They were there for three nights and three days. Trump was in for a shock when he saw the bill. It was $3000, plus $900 for their food. "Why is the food so expensive?" exclaimed Trump. "I didn't even touch your food! I didn't eat a thing."

"It doesn't matter Sir" said the manager "the food was at your disposal and even if you didn't touch it, that's your problem. You owe us $3900."

Trump thought for a while and said "No problem, you now owe me $2100."

"Why is that" wondered the Manager

"I am going to pay you your $3900. We stayed here for three nights, you slept with my wife three times and because I love her so much, I charge $2000 per night. That comes to $6000. If I deduct $3900 from $6000 the balance is $2100" said Trump.

"But I didn't sleep with your wife" exclaimed the manager.

"It doesn't matter, my wife was here at your disposal and if you didn't touch her, that's your problem."

*Trump eventually paid the bill and vowed never to return to that hotel again. They were home again and Trump was killing flies. Melanie never knew that Trump's favorite pass time was killing flies.*

## 176. Fly hunter!!!

Melanie arrived in the kitchen and found her husband with a sophisticated fly killer tool.

"What you doing?"

"I am killing the flies" he replied

"Have you killed any?"

"Yes, three males and two females!"

Intrigued, Melanie asked him "How do you differentiate between the males and the females?"

He replied:

"The males land on beer cans and I always find the females on

the phone."

*Trump and Melanie went shopping. Suddenly Melanie disappeared and he could not find her.*

## 177. Let's go look for your wife

Trump carelessly bumped into a stranger while he was rushing around, frantically looking for Melanie.

The stranger was furious.

"Hey! Can't you look where you going?"

94

"Sorry, I didn't see you there; I was looking for my wife."

"What a coincidence, I am also looking for my wife too! What does your wife look like?"

"She is tall, blue eyes, very good looking, full lipped, long legs and big breasts. She is wearing a transparent shirt and a tight skirt. How about yours, what does she look like?"

"It doesn't matter! Let's rather look for yours."

*He couldn't find her so he went home hoping that she would show up there. On the way, he gave an Indian a lift.*

## 178. Great trade

The Indian was thumbing for a ride on the side of the road.

He stopped the car and the Indian got in.

After a bit of small talk, the Indian noticed a brown bag on the front seat. "What's in the bag?" the Indian asked.

Trump said "It's a bottle of wine. I got it for my wife."

The Indian was silent for a moment then said "Good trade."

*Just as he expected Melanie was at home. She had decided to leave early because of a headache and later that night, they are watching "Who wants to be a millionaire"*

## 179. Is that your last answer?

Melanie went to bed early with a headache. Earlier that night, they had been watching "Who wants to be a millionaire." When Trump joined her, he was in a frisky mood. He asked his wife if she was in the mood as well.

Melanie answered "Not tonight dear, I have a headache." Trump said "Is that your final answer?"

She said "Yes."

"OK, then I'd like to phone a friend," he replied.

*Trump and Melanie started to have their first marital disputes.*

## 180. Who is really related to that cow?

They had been fighting for a few days. Trump thought it would be good to go for a long drive in the country side to help resolve things. Other than the music, there was complete silence. Trump was driving and Melanie was looking out the window indifferently.

Trump noticed that Melanie was looking at some cows grazing in the green field. He took the opportunity to make the situation lighter and asked Melanie: "Relative of yours?" Melanie, breaking the silence instantly replied "Yes, by marriage."

*Their problems and the cold war waged on and by this stage Melanie didn't want to make Trump his coffee.*

## 181. Do it yourself and save time

Trump was complaining about Melanie to a friend. He said "I had been watching my wife's routine at breakfast for years" he explained. "She made lots of trips between the refrigerator, stove and table, often carrying a single item at a time. One day I told her "Hon, why don't you try carrying several things at once?"
"Did it save time?" the friend asked.
"Actually, yes" replied Trump.
"It used to take her twenty minutes to make breakfast."
Now I do it in seven."

*Trump was tired of the problems and the silent treatment from Melanie. He wanted to break up but just didn't know how he was going to do it.*

## 182. Silent treatment

The next week Trump realized that he would need his wife to wake him up at 5:00 am for an early morning business flight to the North Pole. Not wanting to be the first to break the silence, he wrote on a piece of paper "Please wake me at 5:00 Am." and put it on Melanie's side of the bed.

The next morning he woke up, only to discover it was 9:00 am and that he had missed his flight. Furious, he wanted to find out why his wife hadn't woken him when he noticed a piece of paper by the bed; it said "It is 5:00am, wake up."

*To make things even worse, Melanie is thinking of killing her inlaws.*

## 183. Unusual Funeral

Melanie was leaving a convenience store with her morning coffee when she noticed a most unusual funeral procession approaching the nearby cemetery.

A long black hearse was followed by a second long black hearse about fifty feet behind the first one. Behind the second hearse was a solitary woman walking a pit bull on a leash. Behind her, a short distance back, were about two hundred women walking single file. The woman was so curious that she respectfully approached the woman walking the dog and said "I am so sorry for your loss, and I know now is a bad time to disturb you, but I have never seen a funeral like this. Whose funeral is it?"

"My sister in law's" she replied.

"What happened to her?"

The woman replied "My dog attacked and killed her." She inquired further "Well, who is in the second hearse?" The woman answered "My mother-in-law. She was trying to help my sister in law when the dog turned on her." A poignant and thoughtful moment of silence passed between the two women.

"Can I borrow the dog?" said Melanie

"Get in line." replied the woman

*Trump went to visit his Japanese neighbor who was sick. He accidentally finished him off.*

## 184. The oxygen supply

Trump went to visit his Japanese neighbor who was recently involved in a car accident. When he got there, he found his neighbor had pipes connected by plasters all over his body. He couldn't move at all, only his eyes were visible and it appeared that he was sleeping.

Trump sat next to the bed. Suddenly, his neighbor opened his eyes and began to scream loudly "ANATA WA WATASHI NO SANSO PAIPU O FUNDE IRU ANATA WA BAKA"
Then he took his last breath and died.

Trump was upset and these last words stuck in his mind.

At the funeral Trump approached the widow and the mother of the deceased and asked what "ANATA WA WATASHI NO SANSO PAIPU O FUNDE IRU ANATA WA BAKA" meant

His ex neighbor's mother fainted and his widow went into a rage.
Trump asked his mother again, what those words meant.
"You are stepping on my oxygen pipe, you idiot." replied the
furious widow

*After the funeral, Trump went to put some flowers on his mother's grave. On his way back he met someone that he definitely could relate to, in a way.*

## 185. Why did you have to die?

Trump placed some flowers on the grave of his dearly departed
mother and was returning to his car when his attention was diverted
to another man kneeling at a grave. The man seemed to be praying
with profound intensity and kept repeating "Why did you have
to die? Why did you have to die?" Trump approached him and said
"Sir, I don't wish to interfere with your private grief, but this
demonstration of pain is more than I've ever seen before. For
whom do you mourn so deeply? A child? A parent?" The mourner
took a moment to collect himself then replied "My wife's first
husband." He saw another man in the same state as the first one he
had just passed, so again he went to him and asked if he was
mourning his wife. The man replied no; I am mourning for this
man. He owes me money and now I can't get it back.

*In the next couple of weeks, Trump made up with his wife, but she still felt that from time to time he didn't treat her well.*

## 186. Keep the beer coming before the game begins

Trump came home from an exhausting day at work; he plopped
down on the couch in front of the television, and shouted to Melanie
"Get me a beer before it starts." Melanie sighed and brought him a
beer. Fifteen minutes later, he shouted "Get me another beer before
it starts." She was getting angry but got him another beer anyway
and slammed
it down next to him. He finished that beer and a few minutes later
shouted "Quick, get me another beer; it's going to start any
minute." Melanie was now furious.

She shouted at him "Is that all you're going to do tonight? Drink beer and sit in front of that TV? You're nothing but a lazy, drunken, fat slob."

Trump sighed and said "It's started ..."

*Trump's wife went to do his washing while he was watching the game and she came back and attacked him.*

## 187. Your horse is on the phone

Trump was on his couch, watching a soccer game then all of a sudden he was hit on the head and fell to the ground. The poor man stood up, still seeing stars, looked up to see Melanie staring at him. He shouted "are you crazy, why did you hit me?" "It's for the piece of paper I found in your pants where it's written Pallin 049559532" replied Melanie.

"You are an idiot!, those are horse betting numbers; Pallin is the horse's name and 04 is the fourth race, 95 is the amount, 59 is the horse's number, 53 is the type of bet and 2 is the bet time.

Confused she replied "I am sorry, I won't do it again."

Few minutes later, Trump got a knock on the head again. This time he was lying on the floor almost completely unconscious. He screamed out "what's the matter this time?"

Melanie relied "your horse is on the phone."

*Trump's wife, who already had a child, found out she was pregnant again.*

## 188. I am pregnant again

Four years after Melanie and Trump had their first child; Melanie found out that she was pregnant again. She tied up the phone lines telling everyone the good news. The next day, she and her son went shopping. Melanie asked the boy if he was excited about the baby. "Yes" he said. "I know what we're going to name it."

If it is a girl, we're calling her Iva and if it is a boy, we're going to call it quits.

*The time had come for the baby to be born. Melanie had gone into labor and Trump was sitting in the waiting room, waiting to hear the good news.*

## 189. How many babies are you expecting?

The nurse walked into the waiting room and said to the man sitting next to Trump "Congratulations sir, you're the new father of twins!" The man replied "How about that, I work for the Double mint Chewing Gum Company." The man then followed the woman to his wife's room.

About an hour later, the same nurse entered the waiting room and announced that Mr. Smith's wife had just had triplets. Mr. Smith stood up and said "Well, how do you like that, I work for the 3M Company."

The gentleman that was sitting next to him then got up and started to leave. When he was asked why he was leaving, he remarked "I think I need a breath of fresh air."

The man continued "I work for 7-UP."

*Meanwhile Trump's wife just had twins and she was a bit confused.*

## 190. Who is the father of the other twin?

Melanie just gave birth to twins and she was crying, the nurse asked her what was wrong? Are you in any pain?

Melanie replied: No I don't know who the father of the second baby is.

*Melanie had so many kids after that and discovered that she was just too fertile. She wrote a letter to her doctor to see if he could help her with her fertility problem.*

## 191. Application for sterilization

She wrote:

*Dear Doctor*

*I wish to apply for an operation to make me sterile. My reasons are numerous and after being married for seven years and having a child each year, I have come to the conclusion that contraceptives are absolutely useless.*

*After getting married I was told to use the "Rhythm Method." Whilst trying the samba and the tango I got pregnant and I ruptured myself doing the Cha-cha.*

*The doctor then suggested we use the safe period. At this time we were living with the in-laws and we had to wait three weeks for a safe period, when the house was empty. Needless to say this didn't work.*

*A lady of several years experience informed us that if we made love while breast-feeding we would be alright. I finished up with clear skin, silky hair and another child on the way.*

*Another old wife's tale was if I jumped up and down after sex this would prevent pregnancy. After breast-feeding, if I jumped up and down I would have ended up with two black eyes, and even knocked myself unconscious.*

*I asked a chemist about the condom. He demonstrated how easy it was to use so I bought a packet. I fell pregnant again, which doesn't surprise me, as I fail to see how a plastic stretched over the thumb can prevent a baby.*

*I was then supplied with the coil and after many unsuccessful attempts to fit it, we realized that we had to get a left-handed thread and I was definitely a right-handed screw.*

*The Dutch cap came next. We were very hopeful of this as it did not interfere with our sex life at all. But alas, it did give me a severe headache. We were given the largest size, but it was still too tight across my forehead.*

*Finally we tried the pill. At first it kept falling out, then we realized we were doing it wrong. I started then to put it between my knees, thus preventing me from getting anywhere near him. This did work for a while until the night I forgot it, another child resulted.*

*You must appreciate my problem; if this operation is unsuccessful I shall have to revert to oral sex. Although I don't mind just talking about it, it could never be the same as the real thing.*

*Yours faithfully,*
*Melanie Rose*

**Meanwhile Trump's family had an uninvited guest and they were worried about what he might do before leaving. His intensions were not yet clear.**

## 192. Be strong honey, our lives depend on it

An escaped convict, imprisoned for first degree murder, had spent twenty years of his life in prison. While on the run, he broke into Trump's house and tied him and Melanie up in their bedroom. He tied Trump to a chair on one side of the room and his wife to the bed. He got on the bed and climbed right over Melanie and it appeared he was kissing her neck.

Suddenly he got up and left the room. Trump made his way across the room to Melanie, his chair in tow, and whispered "Honey, this guy hasn't seen a woman in years. I saw him kissing you on your neck and then he left in a hurry. Just cooperate and do anything he wants. If he wants to have sex with you, just go along with it and pretend you like it. Whatever you do don't fight him or make him mad. Our lives depend on it. Be strong and I love you."

After spitting out the gag in her mouth, his half naked wife says "Dear, I'm so relieved you feel that way. You're right, he hasn't seen a woman in years, but he wasn't kissing my neck. He was whispering in my ear. He said he thinks you're really cute and asked if we kept the Vaseline in the bathroom. Be strong and I love you too."

*Trump suddenly acquired strength he didn't know he had, he managed to free himself and when the prisoner came out of the bathroom he knocked the prisoner unconscious. Trump then called the police, who congratulated Trump for his service to the community.*

*Trump wanted to avenge the death of his mother, who was killed by Melanie's dog. He took some drastic action.*

## 193. She didn't want to be buried

Trump walked into a bar one day with a badly bruised face, arms and legs. Pence asked him what happened.

Trump replied "I have just come from burying my mother in law! And Pence asked what that had to do with all the bruises he had.

Trump replied "She didn't want to be buried."

## 194. Go to the game or the funeral

A man named, Joe had received a free ticket to the superbowl Finals from his company. Unfortunately, when he arrived at the stadium, he realized the seat was in the last row in the corner of the stadium, he was closer to the Huawei Blimp than the field. About halfway through the first quarter, Joe was looking through his binoculars and saw an empty seat ten rows off the field right on the 50 meter line. He decided to take a chance and make his way through the stadium and around the security guards to the empty seat. As he sat down, Joe asked the gentleman sitting next to him "Excuse me, is anyone sitting here?"

Trump replied "No."

Now, very excited to be in such a great seat for the game, Joe exclaimed to Trump "This is incredible! Who in their right mind would have a seat like this at the Rugby Finals and not use it?" Trump replied "Well, actually, the seat belongs to me. I was supposed to come with my wife. This is the first Final we haven't attended together since we got married."

"Well, that's really sad" said Joe "but still, couldn't you find anyone to take the seat? A friend or close relative?" "No" Trump replied "they're all at my mother in law's funeral."

*Back from the finals, Trump wanted to comfort his wife as she didn't know he was the one who buried her mother alive*

## 195. What type of play do you want?

After the super bowl Finals' party, Trump figured he better spend some quality time with Melanie. He climbed upstairs, walked into the bedroom and crawled into bed. "All right honey" he said "Give me a play you want me to perform."

"How about Foreplay?" his wife replied "What is foreplay?" asked Trump.

"You know" Melanie answered "It happens before the two minute warning."

*The next day, Trump was out partying and there was a*

## 196. Are you drunk or not

A police officer was stalking out a particularly rowdy bar for possibility of people drinking and driving. At closing time, he saw Trump stumble out of the bar, trip on the curb, and try his keys on five different cars before he found his. Then he sat in the front seat fumbling around with his keys for several minutes. Everyone left the bar and drove off. Finally, he started his engine and began to pull away.

The police officer was waiting for him. He stopped Trump, read him his rights and administered the Breathalyzer test. The results showed a reading of 0.0. The puzzled officer demanded to know how that could be. Trump replied "Tonight, I'm the Designated Decoy."

*The policeman still checked Trump in and thought his breathalyzer was not working and kept him in jail for two days, meanwhile his wife was worried and called the police.*

## 197. Is that really your husband?

The police arrived and asked for a description. She told them he's six feet and two inches tall, blonde wavy hair and has a smile that makes everybody love him. The police then went to the next door neighbor to verify this report and the lady next door told the police "You can't believe her. He's five feet and four inches tall, he is bald and he wears a perpetual frown on his face." The neighbor asked Melanie why she gave the police such a false report.

She replied "Just because I reported him missing, doesn't mean I wanted him back."

*Trump finally got out of jail. He invited his new friend that he met in jail to his house. He just told Melanie about the dinner.*

## 198. He is thinking of getting married, we need to show him

"Honey" said Trump "I am bringing a friend home for dinner."

"What, are you crazy? The house is a mess; I haven't been shopping, all the dishes are dirty, and I don't feel like cooking a fancy meal" said Melanie.

"I know all that" said Trump

"Then why did you invite your friend for dinner?" said Melanie

"Because the poor fool is thinking about getting married"
replied Trump.

*Trump's new friend arrived at Trump's house for dinner that night.
He was amazed by the love that still existed between Trump and
Melanie, after so many years of marriage.*

### 199. Honey, what's your name again?

Every time Trump needed something, he preceded his request to his
wife by calling her "My Love", "Darling", "Sweetheart", etc, etc.
His friend looked at him and said "That's really nice after all of
these years you've been married to keep saying those little pet
names." Trump said "Well, honestly, I've forgotten her name."

*After the dinner, they decided to go out, to finish up the night
on a high note.*

### 200. Yuppie, dink and wife

They were all sitting at the bar discussing life.
Trump's friend said "I'm a YUPPIE. You know, Young
Urban Professional."
Trump responded "I'm a DIMK. You know, Double Income
Many Kids."
They then asked Melanie "What are you?"
She replied: "I'm a WIFE. You know Wash, Iron, Fuck, Etc."

*Trump was in the bar and had to relieve himself.*

### 201. Synchronization skills

While sitting at the bar, Trump realized that he desperately needed
to fart. The music was loud so he synchronized his farts with the
music. After two songs, he started feeling better. While drinking his
beer, he realized that everybody was staring at him, but then he
realized that he still had his airpod plugged in.

## 202. Now do what you want

Trump and his friends had spent weeks planning this hunting and fishing trip to the forest. Two Days before they were to leave, Melanie dared him to go and threatened him. The others were disappointed but there was nothing they could do.

Two days later, they reached their camping site to find Trump sitting there next to the tent; he had collected wood already and had some fish on the fire.

"I thought you weren't coming."

"How did you convince your wife to let you come?"

"I've been here since yesterday night. Yesterday afternoon, I was sitting on the couch; Melanie came up behind me and covered my eyes, and said, 'guess who's here?'"

When I turned around I saw her wearing her sexy Lingerie. She took my hand and took me to the bedroom where she had lit dozens of candles and had flowers all over the bed. On the bed she had handcuffs and strings.

So she asked me to handcuff her and tie her to the bed, that's what I did. Then she said 'now do whatever you want'.

... and here I am."

## 203. What would you do if I won the lotto?

"Trump asked her "Honey, Tell me what you would do if I told you that I have won the lotto?

"I will take half and leave you! She replied."

"Great, here's five thousand dollars, now, fuck off."

*He decided to continue playing the lottery and finally he hit the jackpot.*

## 204. I have won the lotto

Trump came home that evening, barged in singing with joy
and called for Melanie.
"Baby!! Baby!! I have won the lotto!!! Pack your bags!!
"Oh baby, that's wonderful, are you taking me on a trip, should
I take the winter or summer clothes?
"Both bitch and you fuck off."

*Melanie refused to leave, but was now serious
about a proper divorce. This would entitle her to a
share of Trump's fortune. Meanwhile she sends
Trump on a trip to the hospital.*

## 205. On target

Unfortunately an unexpected incident sent Trump to the
hospital. Trump was lying in the hospital bed with his head
covered with a huge bandage.
The nurse asked him "Poor sir, your wife must be missing
you?" He replied "She usually does, but this time she got me."

*Melanie finally told Trump, that she wanted a
divorce. Trump was not impressed.*

## 206. The divorce

They went for a drive in Trump's car. They were going sixty
miles an hour on the highway. Trump was driving. Suddenly
Melanie began to speak:
"Listen, I know that we have been married for fifteen years but
I want a divorce."
Trump remained quiet and accelerated to 80 miles an hour.
"I have slept with your best friend and we have become lovers."
Once again Trump remained quiet and accelerated to one
hundred miles per hour.
"I am going to keep the house and the kids" said Melanie.
Again Trump accelerated to a hundred and twenty miles per hour. "I
also want the car and everything in the bank account" she said. The
car was heading for a wall and Trump accelerated to a hundred and
forty miles per hour.

"What about you, what do you want?" she asked
"Nothing, I already have all I need" replied
Trump "What is that?"
"The airbag, Bitch!"

*Melanie survived the crash and Trump is now discussing the divorce with Pence.*

## 207. I am getting a divorce

"I am in a divorce process" he told Pence.
"Really, why?" Pence asked.
"Would you be able to be with someone who drinks, smokes and comes home late?"
"No?" replied Pence.
"Neither would my wife."

*The divorce was finalized and Trump lost almost everything.*

## 208. Poker and marriage has a lot in common

After his divorce Trump realized that poker wasn't the only game that started with holding hands and ending with a staggering financial loss.

*Even though Melanie gained a lot from her divorce, she quickly lost most of it including her newly bought Lamborghini*

## 209. What happened to my Lamborghini?

After the divorce, Melanie was driving down the road in her new, red $300000 Lamborghini. She was cruising at about sixty miles an hour, radio blaring, having a great time. She came up to this trucker whose huge truck was taking up both lanes. To her dislike, he was only going about forty miles an hour. She could not get past so she decided to tailgate him instead. So, she got to within a foot of his rear bumper. The trucker looked back and saw her on his ass, and motioned for her to get off of it, but to her it looked like a wave and she waved back. Since her first attempt was futile, she decided to get a little closer and began flashing her headlights, hopefully making herself more visible in the process. Once again the trucker saw her on his ass, and this time motioned for her to pull over to the side of the road.

The trucker stepped out of his vehicle with a chunk of chalk and drew a circle three feet in diameter in the middle of the road. He instructed her not to move until he told her what to do. Naive as she was, she agreed to it and stepped inside the circle.

The trucker went back to his truck and pulled out a heavy bat. He walked over to the Lamborghini and beat it, and beat it, and beat it again. When he was done, all that is left was a brand new, red $300000, pile of metal. Satisfied, he threw the bat into his truck and walked over to Melanie. When he got there, to his astonishment, she was rolling around on the street laughing hysterically. He asked her "Why are you laughing? I just beat the crap out of your car!!" She was laughing too hard to respond, but between giggles he could only make out "While you weren't looking I stepped out of the circle!"

> *Trump had been paying child support for his last born daughter and now that she was eighteen, he thought that his suffering was over, not knowing that his wife had a surprise in store for him.*

## 210. Child Support

Trump told his daughter Ivanka,

"Give your mother this cheque for child support and tell her it's the last; then take note of her facial expressions."

Ivanka went home and did as he said. Her mom said to her:

"When you see your father, tell him he is not your father, and then take note of HIS facial expressions.

> *After the divorce, Trump met and married another woman but was soon divorced again. He struggled to understand women. Djinna the genie appeared in his life again, maybe he could shed some light on the subject.*

## 211. The complex subject of women

Trump was walking down the road when he unexpectedly slipped on an old lamp; he picked it up and rubbed it clean. When he did this, the genie Djinna appeared and informed Trump that he had reason to rejoice. He said he had been stuck in the lamp for many years and now he had freed him. He was now entitled to a wish that he would fulfill. Trump thought for a while then he said:

"I always dreamed to go to Africa but I have always been afraid of airplanes and the sea; so I would like you to build a bridge from here to Africa so I can drive there and come back.

Djinna was quiet for a moment and then burst out laughing "it's impossible!" Think of the immense structure that would be needed to hold the bridge, all the concrete, steel, restaurants, filling stations, hotels along the way that I would have to build. I am a Genie but I can't do the impossible. Ask me something else that is reasonable" said Djinna. Okay said Trump after thinking for a while, Trump said

"I have been married and divorced three times, my ex-wives have always accused me of not caring much and being insensitive; so I would like to understand women, know what they feel, know what they think when they are silent, know why they cry, what they mean, know how to make them happy and so on..."

Djinna looked at him and said "how many lanes do you want on that bridge, two or four?"

*Trump left for Africa, still without his deepest wish of understanding women being fulfilled...*

*He married many other ladies in his lifetime and Melanie also married many other men and had many more kids.*

# Chapter 8 x Cheating in the couple's lives

*The Trump household was full of cheating and affairs involving both husband and wife. Here are some of the stories that made it to the limelight.*

*When he just started his cheating "career" and felt bad about it, Trump decided to go and confess to clear his mind.*

### 212. Rubbing against is the same as putting it in?

Trump decided to confess to his priest "Father, I almost had an affair with a woman" "What do you mean almost?" questioned the priest. "Well, we got undressed and rubbed against each other, but then I stopped." "Rubbing together is the same as putting it in" explained the priest. "You're not to go near that woman again. Now, say five Hail Mary's and put $50 in the Priest advancement box."

Trump left and said his prayers and then walked over to the priest advancement box, He paused for a moment and then decided to leave. The priest quickly ran over to him and exclaimed "I saw that you didn't put any money in the box!" "Well Father, I rubbed up against it and like you said, it's the same as putting it in!"

*Trump became suspicious of Melanie. People he knew her were telling him that she was cheating on him.*
*At the beginning he did not understand what was going on as can be attested from the following conversation.*

### 213. I think my wife is selling drugs

Trump told Pence "I think my wife is selling drugs! Yesterday I was running a little bit late for work and the phone rang. I answered it. Before I could say anything a male voice on the line said, hey honey is that DOPE gone yet?"

*Trump soon became convinced that his wife was having an affair.*

### 214. Give me some condoms, I am going to your place

A man went into a pharmacy to buy condoms and when he left he was laughing like he was mad. Trump, who was the pharmacist at that time, thought he was a bit crazy but there weren't any laws preventing crazy people from buying condoms. The next day, the man came back to buy condoms and again he left the pharmacy laughing like a mad man. He did this for the next few days and eventually it started to get on Trump's nerves. One day Trump asked his assistant to follow this man after he left the pharmacy. An hour later the assistant returned.
"Did you follow him, where did he go?" asked Trump.
The assistant replied "He went to your house, sir."

*Trump is now certain his wife is cheating on him and the list of her lovers is growing. His friend could actually be one of his wife's lovers.*

### 215. Your wife doesn't want to see me

Pence: My mistress just left me and she doesn't want to see me anymore.
Trump: Come on, let's go eat some fries, you will feel better afterwards.
Pence: I would love to, but every time, after having sex, we used to go out for fries.
Trump: OK then, come to my place and my wife will make us a good coffee.
Pence: I'm telling you, she doesn't want to see me anymore.

*Trump's son told him that the neighbor was sleeping with Melanie.*

## 216. The key of paradise

Trump's boy Junior asked his father "Dad, when you make love to mom, what is she to you?"

Trump, who was surprised at this question, replied "Well, son she is the door of paradise."

Then the boy asked "then what are you to mom?"

Trump replied "I am the key to paradise, my boy."

Then Junior whispered in his ear: Be careful then, I think the neighbor got the same key.

*The dog is finally settling the matter and bringing in Melanie's lovers piece by piece.*

## 217. This dog is a go getter

Trump got a new dog that had a wonderful talent.

Trump was telling Pence "I have a new dog, he is wonderful! I let him sniff a panache of pheasant, he brought me a pheasant. I made him sniff a rabbit skin and he brought me a hare, but when I let him sniff Melanie's panties, he brought me the neighbor's testicles.

*Trump wanted to catch his wife in the act, so he came home early. Due to an unfortunate incident he died and was now at the gates of heaven.*

## 218. How did you die?

At the gates of heaven, Trump was telling his story.

"For a very long time I had suspected my wife of having extra marital relations. I arrived home early one day and as I expected, I found my wife completely naked on the bed. I immediately started searching the apartment to find the guilty person. I searched the entire apartment in vain. I remembered the small balcony outside. I got there and found a man hanging on a rope next to the balcony. I stepped on his hand to make him fall but he held on tightly, so I went inside and found a hammer, came back and hit his hand with all my strength, until finally he let go and fell but unfortunately a tree broke his fall. When I saw that he was still moving, I went back inside to get the fridge, which I threw on top of him and killed him. The shock of it all caused me to have a heart attack, so here I am."

A voice said "You go to hell you don't deserve to go to heaven."
Suddenly another man arrived at the gates of heaven and told the story of his death.

"I was repainting my balcony, when a man hit my hand with a hammer, causing me to fall. After a tree, luckily broke my fall, he threw a fridge on top of me, which caused my death.

The voice said "I heard about you, you may go back to earth."
Just then a third man arrived at the gates. He also told the story of his death.

"I was quietly sitting naked in a fridge, minding my own business and just like that, I ended up here."

> *Luckily Trump was eventually sent back to earth. He hired his Chinese friend Fu who had become a famous private detective to help him catch his wife in the act.*

## 219. Chinese Detective

Fu was to watch Melanie and report any activities that might develop. A few days later, Trump received a report from Fu.
"Most honorable sir,
You leave house.
He come house.
I watch.
He and she leave house.
I follow.
He and she get on train.
I follow.
He and she go in hotel.
I climb tree, look in window.
He kiss she.
She kiss he.
He strip she.
She strip he.
He play with she.
She play with he.
I play with me.
Fall out of tree, no see.
NO FEE."

*Fu was of no use, so Trump thought that he would do a better job of spying on his wife himself. After watching the house from a distance, he saw a man enter his home.*

## 220. That towel is for hands, pig

Trump immediately followed after him into the house and found his wife, sweaty and naked on the bed. He rushed into the bathroom, angrily, to find a man standing there, trying to hide his private parts with a towel.

Trump said "Don't be a pig, that towel is for hands only."

*Now he has proof that his wife was cheating on him. The news that hurt him the most was what he discovered when he brought a robot lie detector machine home.*

## 221. Lie Detector!!!

Trump brought home a robot that was a lie detector machine.

That day his twelve year old son Junior was two hours late from school.

"Where were you all this time?" asked Trump.

"I was in the library preparing for my homework" Junior said.

The robot headed straight to Junior and slapped him.

Trump explained "My son, this robot detects lies! So you better start telling the truth."

"OK.... I was with a friend and we were watching a movie: The Ten Commandments"

Whack, the robot slapped Junior again.

"OK, it was a porn movie" said Junior.

"You should be ashamed of yourself son, when I was your age I never lied to my parents."

Whack! The robot slapped Trump.

Melanie laughed and teasingly said to Trump "He really is your son ....."

Whack! The robot slapped Melanie.

*He soon discovered that his wife was also involved with his friend and that is what started Trump's cheating spree. Now confused and angry, he decided to finally start cheating as well, so he went to Thailand to find a girlfriend so no one will find out.*

## 222. It's me before the operation

Trump went to a lady's apartment after having seduced her. When the girl opened the door, he immediately went to her bedroom hoping for some action but a large portrait of a man in the room caught his attention and caused him to feel nervous.

"Is that your husband? He is going to kill me"

"NO, no, I am not married."

"Is it your dad or brother? He is going to kill me."

"No, my dad passed away a long time ago and I don't have a brother."

"Who is it then?"

"It's me before the operation."

*That first experience made him go back to the US and try to find a girl there and he was becoming increasingly bold with his affairs. He brought some of his concubines home when his wife was out and he was almost caught once; fortunately for him his wife did not connect the dots.*

## 223. I am having a heart attack

Melanie came home from her shopping, only to hear weird noises coming from her bedroom. She opened the door to find Trump naked, lying on the bed, sweating.

"What's going on? She asked.

"I am having a heart attack" replied Trump.

Melanie ran to her phone and began calling an ambulance. While she was dialing, Junior began shouting "Mom, mom, Aunt Danny is hiding in your wardrobe and she is naked."

Melanie immediately hung up the phone and ran back into her bedroom; she opened the wardrobe and found her sister there, completely naked and curled up on the floor.

"You bitch" she said. "My husband is having a heart attack and you're playing hide and seek with the kids."

*At work Melanie told the story about her husband nearly having a cardiac arrest. Her friend, who was not so naive, said that Trump was probably cheating on her. Melanie immediately raced home in an attempt to catch her husband cheating on her but she and Danny died in the process; just like Trump died while trying to catch her cheating.*

## 224. If you checked the fridge, we would still be alive

Melanie and Danny appeared at the gates of heaven at the same time. Melanie asked Danny:

"How did you die?"

"I froze to death" she replied

"Oh, that must have been terrible! How did it feel to freeze to death?" said Melanie

"Well, you shiver a lot, your ears, fingers and toes hurt and after a while you become very calm like you were sleeping... how about you how did you die?"

"Me, I died of a heart attack. I suspected my husband of cheating, so I came home early one afternoon, barged into the house, found my husband watching the news, I ran to the bedroom and found it was empty then I checked the cellar, still empty, then as I was running to check the second floor, I had a heart attack and died. Danny replied "If only you checked the freezer, we would both still be alive."

*Melanie was sent back to earth because the gate keeper felt that it was not her time to go.*

*After she had recovered, her husband decided to take her out. Two incidents took their marriage to an almost open relationship status.*

## 225. You must listen to kids

Junior came home from school and said to his mother "I need to tell you something. On my way back from school, I saw dad in his car next to the woods and ..."

"Listen Son, I don't have time right now, tell me later!" "Mom, Dad was with Aunt Danny and ..."

"I am telling you, I am busy, you can tell me tonight at dinner."

Trump came back from work and everybody sat down at the table for dinner. Melanie said "Son, what did you want to tell me when you came back from school?"

"I saw Dad in his car with Aunt Danny next to the woods and he was removing his pants and she removed her dress and she did to him what you used to do to Uncle Bernie when dad was at work."

## 226. She is my mistress and you are my wife

Trump and Melanie were having dinner in a very classy restaurant.
A very pretty lady walked into the restaurant and went straight up
to Trump and gave him a very long and tender kiss. She told him
that they were going to meet later. Then she left.
Melanie gave him an angry look.
 "Who was that?" She asked, angrily.
"Her? She's my mistress."
"Well, this is the cherry on top! I want a divorce."
"Listen, I understand your anger, but remember you have to realize
that if we divorce, you won't be able to afford all your trips, all
your shopping around the world, all your summer holidays in the
beach, all your winter trips in the mountain, all your expensive cars
and extravagant dresses but it's your decision and I will respect it."
At the same time, Pence walked into the restaurant with a very
beautiful lady.
"Who is that with Pence?" Melanie asked.
"That's his mistress."
"Well, at least ours is more beautiful." Retorted Melanie

*Now that Trump's affairs were out in the open, he went wild
and is now taking his mistresses in fancy shopping trips
around the world.*

## 227. The cheque bounced

Trump arrived at Cartier, Place Vendome in Paris with a beautiful
young lady. Together they choose a necklace worth fifty thousand
dollars for her. It was time to pay and Trump brought out his
cheque book and wrote out a cheque for Fifty thousand dollars. The
shop owner was not comfortable taking a cheque. Trump realized
that the shop owner was not comfortable and reassured him
"I have the feeling that you think the cheque will bounce?" said
Trump.
"Yes" said the shop owner.
"Alright here is what we are going to do. Today is Saturday, my
bank is already closed. I would like you to keep the cheque and the
necklace. Monday when you clear the cheque, you can deliver the

necklace to the lady's address, okay."

"The shop owner, who was reassured, happily agreed to this and even undertook to deliver the necklace himself free of charge."

Monday, when he tried to clear the cheque, as expected the cheque bounced.

Angrily he phoned Trump.

"It's not such a big deal! You didn't lose a cent and I got to enjoy the lady's company the entire weekend! Thanks for your assistance and no hard feelings."

*While he was away for the weekend, his wife decided to also go and have some fun, she went to her neighbor.*

## 228. I am feeling wild tonight!!!

Melanie knocked on her neighbor's door. When he opened the door, she said:

"I am feeling very wild tonight, I want to get drunk, have fun and make love the whole night; are you doing anything tonight?"

"No!" exclaimed the neighbor excitedly.

"Great, then can you look after my dog?" asked Melanie.

*After the weekend away, Trump decided to visit a nudist beach in South Africa that one of his mistresses had told him about. He decided to take Melanie and a South African kid he was trying to adopt.*

## 229. The nudist camp

This was the first time the boy had been to a nudist beach. He was very interested and asked Melanie many questions.

"Mom, why do some women have bigger breasts than you?"

Feeling embarrassed, Melanie replied "Well, you see, the bigger your breasts are, the less intelligence you have."

"Ah, oh I see; thanks" said her son.

Later on the boy came back to find out more.

"Mom, why do some men have a bigger penis than dad?"

Feeling embarrassed, again she replied:

"Well it's the same with women, the bigger a man's penis, the less intelligent he is."

After a while Melanie noticed that Trump was missing.

"Have you seen your dad?" Melanie asked her son.

"Yes, he is behind that rock over there talking to the most stupid lady here and the more he speaks to her, the more stupid he becomes."

*Trump and Melanie got into an argument on the beach so Trump decided to leave, leaving Melanie behind.*

## 230. How did I get here?

Trump leaving Cape Town and was driving towards Stellenbosch. On the way he picked up a lady hitch hiker who was wearing a very short skirt.

Just when he got to Stellenbosch, Trump accidentally touched the woman's leg by mistake when he was changing gears. The woman looked him in the eyes and whispered "You can go further, you know."

So Trump drove all the way to Durban.

*When Trump reached Durban, he took advantage of the warm weather and went to the beach.*

## 231. James Bond

Trump was taking a walk when he bumped into a young lady. He then kept looking at his watch. The girl asked him "Why are you looking at your watch, do you have an appointment?"

He replied "No, the watch is talking to me." "What is it saying to you?"

"It is telling me that you are not wearing underwear."

"It is wrong as I am wearing underwear" she said.

"Well my watch is one hour forward, so let's go for a walk."

*While going from one lady to another, his dating career was ended by two events; the first one is where he lost one of his testicles.*

## 232. Chinese Torture

Trump went to visit his friend Fu. Fu said to him "You may stay in my home but if you lay a finger on my daughter, I will inflict upon you the three worst Chinese tortures known to man." "OK" said Trump, thinking that his daughter must be pretty old.

During dinner, Fu's daughter came downstairs. She was young, beautiful, and had a fantastic body. She was obviously attracted to Trump as she couldn't keep her eyes off him during the meal. Remembering the old man's warning, he ignored her and went up to bed alone. During the night, he could bear it no longer and snuck into her room for a night of passion. He was careful to keep everything quiet, so the old man wouldn't hear. Near dawn, he crept back to his room, exhausted but happy.

He woke to feel a pressure on his chest. Opening his eyes, he saw a large rock on his chest with a note on it that read 'Chinese Torture 1: Large rock on chest.' "Well, that's pretty crappy" he thought. "If that's the best the old man can do, then I don't have much to worry about." He picked the boulder up, walked over to the window, and threw the boulder out.

As he did so, he noticed another note on it that read 'Chinese Torture 2: Rock tied to left testicle.' In a panic he glanced down and saw the rope that was already getting close to taut. Figuring that a few broken bones were better than castration, he jumped out of the window after the boulder.

As he plummeted towards the ground, he saw a large sign on the ground that read 'Chinese Torture 3: Right testicle tied to bed post.'

*The second event broke his heart and sealed his fate...*

## 233. A suitcase full of dollar's for your services

Trump traveled back to Africa to relive the experience he had in South Africa and decided to go to the DRCongo this time and stay there for a month. Once there, he decided to hire a prostitute for a month and agreed to pay her when he is about to leave. He put the dollars he was going to pay her in a suitcase, which he showed her. So at the end of his stay, he gave the prostitute the suitcase at the airport, they said their goodbye's, even though they spoke different languages. Trump waited until he got on the plane before he called to the prostitute and shouted:

"hee, hee, el fakee dollaress" informing her that the dollars in the suitcase were fake

The prostitute was upset and just as he was about to enter the plane she called to him too and shouted:

"hee, heee, all AIDS contaminatreeee" informing him that she had given him AIDS.

*After this bad experience, he decided that from now on, he would be faithful to his wife but she would have to be faithful as well. When he arrived back, he took a taxi home.*

## 234. What would you do?

He got back a day earlier than expected. It was after midnight. While on route home, he asked the taxi driver to be a witness for him. Trump suspected his wife was with someone and he intended to catch her in the act. For $100, the taxi driver agreed. Quietly arriving at the house, Trump and the taxi driver tiptoed into Melanie's bedroom. Trump switched on the lights, yanked the blanket back and there was his wife in bed with another man.

Trump put a gun to the naked man's head. The wife shouted: "Don't do it! This man has been very generous. I lied when I told him I had inherited a lot of money. He paid for the Corvette I bought for you. He paid for our new Cruiser. He paid for our house at the lake. He paid for our country club membership and he even paid for some of our monthly expenses."

Shaking his head from side-to-side, Trump slowly lowered the gun.

He looked over at the taxi driver and said "What would you do?"

The taxi driver said "I'd cover his ass up with that blanket before he catches a cold."

*They decided to be faithful, but it seemed that Trump did not learn his lesson and was still attracted by the life of plentiful mistresses, that he used to live.*

## 235. Give the lady a kiss

Melanie was on her way to drop off Junior at school. On the way, they bumped into Melanie's friend who happened to be very beautiful. "Son, give my friend a kiss hello" said Melanie.

"No mom."

"Come on son, just do it."

"No mom."

"Don't start acting up! Why don't you want to give her a kiss?" "Because dad tried yesterday and he got a Klap."

# Chapter 9 X Trump is overwhelmed and goes crazy

*There were many events in Trump's life and career that hinted on his mental situation and at the end contributed towards him losing his mind.*

*At the time when Trump was a pharmacist:*

## 236. Does the Viagra work?

A lady walked into his pharmacy.
She asked Trump "Do you have Viagra?"
"Yes" he answered.
She asked "Does it work?"
"Yes" he answered.
"Can you get it over the counter?" she asked.
Trump replied "I can if I take two."

*When Trump and his mates were construction workers; they were working on a project to install poles for the city. Some of them were already showing sign of mental deficiency.*

## 237. Poles

A man stopped at a Gas station to fill up his tank. He then decided to buy a drink at the station's store. He was inside the store when he noticed two guys, digging, on the other side of the road. Trump was digging a two meter hole and Pence was filling in the hole once it was dug. The stranger watched this process going on for a while; intrigued, he decided to find out what they were doing. He went up to them and asked:

"Hey, I have been watching you guys from the store across the road and I was wondering, what is the point of what you guys are doing?"
"It is very simple, you will understand, usually we are a team of three. The third man's job is to plant the poles inside the hole before I close it up, but he is sick today. Being responsible workers, we decided carry on without him." said Trump

*Trump was on his way to Russia for a business trip.*

## 238. I don't want to be up here the whole day
Trump and Pence were together on the plane. After two hours of flying, the pilot announced over the intercom that they had just lost an engine but it was all right because they had three more but it would increase flying time by one hour. Half an hour later, the pilot announced that they had just lost another engine but it was all right because they had two more left and that the flight would just take an extra half an hour. Trump leaned over and said to Pence "If we lose the last two engines, we will be up here all day."

*Once they reached their destination, they went to a bar for a drink and caused the barman to lose a lot of money.*

## 239. When I drink, everyone drinks. Who's paying?
The barman asked Trump "What would you like to drink?" Trump replied "When Trump drinks, everyone drinks."
The barman was amazed by Trump's generosity and served everyone a drink. Half an hour later, Trump finished his drink and said "When Trump drinks, everyone drinks."
The barman was thinking this guy is really generous and served him and everyone else a second round.
After many rounds like that, the barman commented to Trump
"Sir, you must keep in mind that the bill is already $1000" Trump replied "When Trump pays, everyone pays."

*Trump went to the rest room before leaving the bar.*

## 240. What you up to? Same thing you're up to

The first toilet door was closed so he went to the second one.
As soon as he sat down, he heard someone say
"Hi! How are you doing?"
Surprised, he told himself that this was not really the best place
to chat, but he decided not to care.
"Yeah, I am okay thank you" he replied sheepishly.
"What you up to?" said the voice again.
"Well, the same as you, just taking a dump" replied Trump.
Then he heard the voice say:
"Listen, I'll have to call you back later, I can't hear a thing you
are saying, there's some loud idiot in the next cubicle, butting in."

*The next day, Trump had a meeting and he decided
to walk to it. As he was unfamiliar with the place,
he got lost. He wandered around, lost for hours but
suddenly he desperately needed to take a dump in
the most urgent way.*

## 241. If you drop it, I will drop you

He eventually came across a house that was under construction. He
walked in hurriedly, noticing that it appeared to be empty. He sat
in the middle of what seemed to be the future living room and he
was about to relieve himself. The first bomb was on the way and it
was about to drop on the ground. He had is eyes looking down and
when he looked up, he saw a Russian police man who happened to
be the owner of the house pointing a gun at him.
"If that bomb falls on the living room, you will also fall" he said
Immediately, trump recalled his bomb and it went straight back in
and he wore his pant back.
Trump left the house and the urgency to shit completely vanished.

*When Trump returned from his trip, his family
decided that he needed treatment for his mental
condition as well as rehabilitation for vodka
addiction. They called a mental institution to enquire
about an appointment for Trump. What they heard
was a message on an answering machine.*

## 242. Answering Service at the Mental Institute

Hello, and welcome to the mental health hot line.

If you are obsessive-compulsive, press 1 repeatedly.

If you are co-dependent, please ask someone to press 2 for you.

If you have multiple personalities, press 3, 4, 5, and 6.

If you are paranoid, we know who you are and what you want. Stay on the line so we can trace your call.

If you are delusional, press 7 and your call will be transferred to the mother ship.

If you are schizophrenic, listen carefully and a little voice will tell you which number to press.

If you are manic depressive, it doesn't matter which number you press, no one will answer.

If you have a nervous disorder, please fidget with the hash key until someone comes on the line.

If you are dyslexic, press 6969696969.

If you have amnesia, press 8 and state your name, address, phone number, date of birth, social security number, and your mother's maiden name.

If you have post-traumatic-stress disorder, slowly and carefully press 000.

If you have bipolar disorder, please leave a message after the beep, or before the beep, or after the beep. Please wait for the beep.

If you have short-term memory loss, press 9. If you have short term memory loss, press 9. If you have short term memory loss, press 9. If you have short term memory loss, press 9.

If you have low self esteem, please hang up. All our operators are too busy to talk to you.

*On his way to the institution, he got into an accident and almost died along with the people who were taking him to the institution.*

## 243. Through which whole did it go

Three people, including Trump died. They all went directly to the gates of heaven and were about to cross to the other side, when they were questioned. The first one was a computer specialist, the second one was a mathematician, and the third one was Trump,

Who was mentally disturbed at the time of his death. The gatekeeper said "I will give you the chance to avoid going to hell."

"You will all get a chance to ask me a question and if I can't answer, I will let you go back to earth." The computer specialist put a complex virus onto the gatekeeper's personal computer and asked him to remove it. The gatekeeper removed the virus with ease and sent the computer specialist to hell.

The mathematician wrote a super complex equation and asked the gatekeeper to solve it. He solved the equation with ease and sent the mathematician to hell.

Trump asked the gatekeeper to bring a chair and drill holes into the seat of the chair then Trump removed his pants and farted on the chair. "Through which hole did my fart go?" asked Trump.

The gatekeeper thought for a minute and said "The third line, 6th hole" answered the gatekeeper

Trump said "No, it went through my asshole."

*So Trump was sent back to earth and checked into the mental institution. Half way through his treatment, the parrot Twitter and another parrot, were also checked in for mental problems.*

### 244. The mad man and the two parrots

The two parrots escaped from the mental institution. Twitter was red and the second parrot was green. The parrots hid in a tree. The manager of the institution asked Trump to fetch the parrots. Trump climbed up the tree and only brought back the red parrot Twitter. The manager asked why he didn't bring the other one too. Trump replied "Isn't it clear, that one is not ripe yet."

*Trump and Pence were in the institution together; they were tired of the institution and wanted to escape to get back to their lives.*

### 245. Escape from the mental institution

"If the guard is on the right, we leave through the left side and if he is on the left, we leave through the right side" said Trump.

"OK", said Pence

During their escape attempt, the two met at the gate and looked at each other with disappointment.
"Ah shit, we can't get out, the guard isn't here."

*The next day, they decided to try to escape when the guard was sleeping.*

## 246. Miaou! Miaou!

It was time to escape and Pence was in front. He was about to jump over the wall of the institution when a brick fell to the ground. The guard shouted "Who's there?
Pence replied "Miaou! Miaou"
The guard thought it was a cat. When Trump was about to jump over the wall, another brick fell to the ground.
Again the guard asked "Who's there?" Trump replied "The second cat!!!"

*They finally escaped as they were so annoying that the guard decided to let them go.*

## 247. Crazy or not that crazy

They had been walking for hours to get back home. When night fell they had no choice, but to sleep outside. They were arguing about where the best place for them to sleep was.
"We should sleep under that tree there" said Trump
"Believe me, we would be safer in the middle of the road" argued Pence.
After a long argument, Trump reluctantly agreed to sleep in the middle of the road.
When they settled down in the middle of the road a car came towards them. It was traveling at a very high speed and swerved to miss them at the very last moment, hitting a tree.
Pence said "See, I told you we would be safer here."

*They police investigated the accident. Trump and Pence were proven to be responsible for the accident and were sent back to the institution. After a while Trump was tested to see if he had been cured on his insanity.*

## 248. Are you still mad or not

With the first test, Trump and some other patients were each put in a bus that does not work and they were told to drive. They were told to call passengers to their busses and tell them the destination of the bus. All the patients "driving" their busses, started calling people and telling them to jump into their bus. Trump was quiet and it seemed that he was not playing along with the exercise. It looked like he was no longer mad and that he understood that these busses could not be driven. The doctor approached Trump and asked him why he was not calling people to his bus. Trump replied "Well, I am waiting for my boy who went to buy Gas, as I just ran out of Gas, so I am stuck here."

Pence had to pass another type of test. The doctor gave Pence and his group delicate hand held fans to cool themselves with, as it was hot. They were told to be gentle with the fans and not to damage them. The next day the doctor came to check whose fan was not destroyed. Only Pence's one was still in one piece. The doctor thought this was a sign that he was cured and asked him how he managed not to destroy his fan. Pence replied "These people are mad, instead of fanning myself like them, I found it easier to hold the fan still and move my head from side to side instead."

*Finally Trump and Pence were cured and were about to be released from the institution but first, the doctor wanted them to address all the new comers who had drug problems and convince them about the bad side effects and consequences of using drugs.*

## 249. Why you should stay away from drugs

"You have been cured of your addiction problem, so tomorrow I want you to talk to all the newcomers about the dangers of using drugs and alcohol. You will try to convince them to stop taking these things. Then you will report back to me."

The next day, the doctor asked them about the newcomers. "Pence, what was your result?"

"Forty three of the new comers vowed to stop using drugs" said Pence

"That's good news, how did you do it?"

"I drew a big O and a small o and I told them, you see the big O; that is your brain before you start smoking and you see the small o; that is your brain after two years of taking drugs."

The doctor asked Trump "What was your result?"

"Two hundred and twelve of the newcomers vowed to stop using drugs" answered Trump.

"How did you convince them?" said the doctor.

"The same thing, I drew a small o and a big O and I told them if you take drugs you will go to jail. The small o is your asshole before you go to jail and the big O is your ass hole after two years in jail.

# Chapter 10 x Old Age, Death and after the death of Trump

*Trump was old now and wanted to live a peaceful quiet life for the rest of his days. This is why he remarried Melanie. They were settling back together and their youngest daughter was asking why they got divorced in the first place, but Melanie didn't want to discuss it.*

### 250. Everything is on the ID card

Their youngest daughter who was nine years old, asked Melanie "How old are you, mom?"

"That is not a question to ask my dear" replied Melanie.

"How tall are you mom?"

"That is not important my dear" replied Melanie.

"Why did you and dad divorce, mom?" asked the girl.

"That is none of your concern my dear" replied Melanie, ending the discussion.

The girl asked her friend why adults don't speak about those things. Her friends told her that the answers to all their questions were in their mom's ID cards.

The next day the girl searched through Melanie's bag and found her ID card; she was glad to see that her friend was right.

She went to Melanie and told her that she now knew her age.

"How old am I?" asked Melanie.

"You are fifty three" said the girl

"I also know how tall you are" she said.

"How tall?" asked Melanie.

" 5'10" " replied the girl

"And I also know why you and dad

divorced." "Why?" asked Melanie

"Because you got an F for sex and that's not a good mark."

*Trump was talking to his children. He was discussing his marriage to their mother and how happy they had been.*

## 251. Twenty five years of happiness

Trump told his sons "Your mom and I were very happy for twenty five years."
"And then?" they asked
"Then we met."

*Trump was glad to be back in his young children's lives again and he looked at his little girl playing and she seemed so innocent but maybe looks can be deceiving.*

## 252. None of that crap here

Trump was watching Ivanka playing in the garden; He smiled as he reflected on how sweet and innocent his little girl was. Suddenly she just stopped and stared at the ground. He went over to her and noticed she was looking at two spiders mating.

"Dad, what are those two spiders doing?" she asked. "They're mating" Trump replied.

What do you call the spider on top, Daddy?" she asked. "That's a Daddy Longlegs." Her father answered. "So, the other one is Mommy Longlegs?" the little girl asked.

"No" Trump replied. "Both of them are Daddy Longlegs."

Ivanka thought for a moment, then took her foot and stomped them flat and said "Well, it might be OK somewhere else but we're not having any of that crap here."

*Trump realized that his children were becoming more aware. He had to deal with the fact that they were beginning to ask questions.*

## 253. What are the dogs doing?

Trump and his youngest daughter were taking a walk in the park, one beautiful spring day. The birds were singing and the sun was shining. On their way they met a couple of dog's mating. Trump was uncomfortable with the scene in front of his daughter and tried to hide the scene from her but she was already aware of the situation, so she asked "Dad, what are those dogs doing?

Feeling more uncomfortable, Trump tried to find an explanation that would protect his innocent young daughter.

" Oh..er..well, you see, its mommy dog and daddy dog, talking a walk and daddy dog got tired, so mommy dog is letting him rest on her back."

"Oh, okay... so to thank her, he is fucking her?"

*It was dinner time and one of Trump's sons was thinking of joining the army, he was the laziest of Trump's kids and everyone was a bit skeptical.*

## 254. A lazy recruit in the army

Trump's son was thinking of joining the army but he was the laziest of Trump's kids.

As the family gathered for a big dinner together, Trump's son announced that he had just signed up at an army recruiter's office. There were audible gasps around the table then some laughter, as his older brothers shared their disbelief that he could handle this new situation. "Oh, come on, quit joking" snickered one. "You didn't really do that, did you?" "You would never get through basic training" scoffed another. The new recruit looked to his mother for help, but she was just gazing at him. When she finally spoke, she simply asked "Do you really plan to make your own bed every morning?"

*Trump was at work when he phoned home. He could not believe his wife was cheating on him again or maybe she was not.*

## 255. You don't have an uncle D. Wrong number?

"Hello, it's Dad here; please will you call your mother to the phone? "I can't, she is upstairs in her room with Uncle D" replied the daughter.

There was a moment of silence.

"But my dear, you don't have an uncle D."

"Of course I do, he is in the room with mom" she said.

"Well, OK, here is what I want you to do. Put the phone aside, run upstairs and knock on the door and shout to your mom and uncle D that Dad's car just arrived in the driveway.

"OK Dad."

A few seconds later, the girl came back crying "I did what you told me."

"So what happened?"

"Mom started screaming, jumped off the bed naked and started running all over the place, she slipped and fell on the side of the bed, she is not moving and I think she is dead."

"Oh God! God! And uncle D?"

"He jumped off the bed naked too and started running all over the place then jumped in the pool through the window, he forgot that you emptied the pool last week to clean it. I think he is dead too."

A moment of silence then Trump said: "The pool, what pool?"

*One of Trump's children had just started college and asked his father for advice on which bank would be best for him to use. Trump recommended him to open an account at BB bank, but later on the boy thought his father gave him some bad advice.*

## 256. Insufficient Funds

Junior came running in tears to his father. "Dad, you gave me some terrible financial advice!"

"I did? What advice was that?" said Trump.

"You told me to put my money in that big bank, and now that big bank is in trouble."

"What are you talking about? That's one of the largest banks in the country" he said. "There must be some mistake."

"I don't think so" he sniffed. "They just returned one of my cheques with a note saying, 'Insufficient Funds'."

*Trump had to explain how banks work to his son. He also needed him to take his dog to this new veterinary in Russia as he was able to make dogs talk.*

## 257. Is the dog talking yet?

Trump had a dog that he was crazy about. He was very proud of his dog. One day he read in the paper, that in Russia, there was a clinic that performed a surgical operation on dogs which enabled them to talk and it cost $5000.

He asked Junior to take the dog to Beijing for this special treatment. Junior was very happy to take the dog to Beijing. Trump gave him the $5000 for the operation, but once he got there, he spent all the money quickly and now wondered how he was going to tell his father, that he had spent all the money and the dog had not had the operation.

Junior went to a restaurant and placed his order, while he thought about the situation he was in. He thought that maybe it would be better if he never returned home.

He decided to tell his father, so he phoned him.

"It has been four days since I last heard from you. How is the dog?" said Trump.

"The dog is fine" said Junior

"So is the dog speaking already?"

"Yeah, he can't stop talking and talking, so are you still sleeping with your secretary?"

"Who told you that?"

"The dog, of course"

"Give it away before you come back, and try to meet some high profile Russian instead" said Trump.

*Ivanka followed in her mother's footsteps, she began to date at an early age, which became apparent to Trump, when he was working as a pharmacist.*

## 258. My dad is a pharmacist

Jarred went to the pharmacy, where Trump worked, to buy condoms. Due to the wide selection that the pharmacy had, he decided to ask for Trump's advice. Trump showed him the different types. Jarred proudly said "I have to meet my new girl friend's parents tonight and after that, we will celebrate. I have a feeling that tonight is the night. She is hot and I intend to have a hot night, if you know what I mean (winking at Trump). I am going to take the twelve pack of condoms please."

That night, he arrived at his girlfriend's house and he was very quiet and reserved during the entire dinner; keeping his eyes on his plate. At the end of the dinner, Ivanka leaned over to the boy and whispered "I didn't know you where this shy."

Jarred replied "I didn't know your father was a pharmacist."

*Straight after dinner, Trump banished Jarred from his house and told him that if he saw him with his daughter again, he would shoot him. A few weeks later, she came with news that shocked Trump and Trump was about to kill someone, unless....*

## 259. Don't sleep with my daughter unless

Ivanka came home one morning and told Trump and
Melanie:
"Dad, mom, I have slept with a man and I am pregnant."
Trump went crazy and went to fetch his gun. He asked her who did this to her, so he could finish him off.
She pleaded "But he is a good guy dad, he is going to take care of his responsibilities."
Just then an MM parks in front of their house and an elegantly dressed Jarred steps out.
He greets Trump and Melanie and says "I have slept with your daughter and I would like to end my relationship with her.
However I am a man of honor and I will make sure that your daughter and the baby are well taken care of. Here is what I propose"
"If it is a girl, I will open a bank account in her name and put in a million dollars. I will also open up ten hairdressing salons across the country for her."
"If it is a boy, I will open a bank account in his name, put a million dollars in and open fifty McDonald franchises across the country for him."
"On the other hand if she loses the baby..." Trump puts his hand on Jarred's shoulder interrupting him "Then you will sleep with my girl again."
*As Trump got back with Melanie, they plan a trip away, back to their honeymoon hotel. Trump makes a mistake with his email once there and some poor widow is now thinking about a fast approaching end.*

## 260. An e-mail from my dead husband

Trump and Melanie were planning a trip to the same hotel where they had stayed on their honeymoon twenty years ago.
But at the last minute, due to unforeseen circumstances,
Melanie couldn't go on Thursday as planned. So they decided that

Chapter 10 Old age, death and after the death of Trump

Trump would go on Thursday and Melanie would meet him the next day. Trump arrived at the hotel, as planned and after checking in; he noticed that in the room they now had a computer with an internet connection. He decided to send Melanie an e-mail, but he made a mistake while typing the e-mail address and sent it to the wrong person.

A recently widowed woman who had just arrived home from her husband's funeral, who had passed away, due to a cardiac arrest, read the e-mail. After reading the e-mail, she fainted. Junior found his mother lying on the floor, unconscious, under the computer. He read the opened e-mail.

*To my dear wife,*

*I have arrived safely. You will be surprised to hear from me now and especially in this way. Here, they have computers now and you can send messages to those you love. I just got here and checked that everything is ready for you tomorrow.*

*I can't wait to see you and hope your trip will be as smooth as mine. Ps: It is not necessary for you to bring many clothes as it is hot as hell here.*

**Trump and Melanie had been married for twenty years and recently remarried, Melanie is now pregnant. Every time they were making love since their remarriage, Trump insisted that they do it in the dark. Melanie wanted to find out why Trump insisted on the lights being off.**

## 261. I will tell you about the vibrator, if you tell me about the kids

One night, in the middle of their deed, she switched on the lights and looked down, she saw Trump holding a long modern vibrating dildo. Bastard, she screamed, how could you lie to me all these years?

Trump looked her straight in her eyes and replied

"If I explain about the toy you must explain about the pregnancy"

**Trump was watching TV with his wife and there was a bit of a weird vibe between them. A program came on that could save Trump's life.**

## 262. Touch the TV and you will be cured

Trump and Melanie were watching a miraculous therapy show on TV. The magician in the show said, if the viewers at home wanted to be healed, place one hand on the television set and the other hand on the body part where they wanted to be healed. Melanie got up and slowly hobbled to the television set, placed her right-hand on the television set and her left hand on her arthritic shoulder that was causing her to have great pain.

Then Trump got up, went to the television and placed his right hand on the TV and his left hand on his crotch.

Melanie scowled at him and said "I guess you just don't get it. The purpose of doing this is to heal the sick, not to raise the dead."

*Trump wanted to cure all his ailments, so Melanie and their son accompanied him to a world class hospital in Cuba where he could be healed. While visiting their doctor, they were amazed by a magic wall.*

## 263. The Magical wall

They were amazed by almost everything they saw in Cuba. Melanie went off to do some shopping, while Trump and Junior wandered around. Trump and Junior were particularly amazed by the two metal, shiny silver walls that parted halfway and then closed themselves together again. Junior asked "what is this, dad?" Trump, not having ever seen this before, replied "son, I have never seen this contraption before; I have no idea what it is." While the Junior and his dad were admiring this contraption, an old lady in a wheel chair rolled herself between the two walls when they parted and pressed a button. The walls closed again. Trump and Junior watched intently as small circles of lights, with numbers above the walls, lit up. The walls opened again to reveal a very pretty, young lady, who stepped out of the contraption.

Trump not able to remove his eyes form the girl whispered to Junior "quick, go get your mom."

*Unfortunately the magical wall was not able to transform Melanie from old to young as it was only a Cuban style elevator. They continued with their visit to the hospital. Melanie and Trump had been experiencing memory loss*

*So they visited a memory doctor who sent them both on a power memory class, where they were taught to remember things by association. The treatment seemed to help Trump and he was telling an old friend about it.*

## 264. What is my wife's name again?

A few days after the class, Trump was outside talking with his neighbor about how much the class had helped him.
"What was the name of the Instructor?" asked the neighbor. "Oh, ummmm, let's see," Trump pondered. "You know that flower, you know, the one that smells really nice but has those prickly thorns, what's that flower's name?"
"A rose?" offered the neighbor.
"Yes, that's it" replied Trump. He then turned toward his house and shouted "Hey, Rose, what's the name of the Instructor we took the memory class from?"

*Trump and Melanie went for their annual medical check-up. Trump was telling the doctor all about the miracles that was happening in his life.*

## 265. So many miracles in my life these days

"As usual, there is nothing to worry about" said the doctor. "How do you manage to stay this fit, it's amazing?"
"It's because God is taking care of me" replied Trump. "Let me tell you what happened yesterday, I went to the toilet for an urgent matter and the light switched on by itself and when I was done, the light went off by itself. Isn't that proof that God is watching over me?"
"Of course" said the Doctor not wanting to contradict him. "Put your clothes back on and wait in the waiting room while I check your wife." Melanie then came in.
"Good morning Melanie!" Tell me, is Trump losing his mind? He just told me that when he went into the bathroom the lights went on automatically and then they automatically went off when he had finished."
"Ah, the idiot!" said Melanie irritably. "He's urinating in the fridge again."

## 266. Unwanted proof

She was buying some dog food, she went to pay for it and the cashier said that she couldn't buy the dog food, because she needed to prove that she had a dog. So Melanie went home and brought her dog with her. She was then allowed to buy the dog food. The next day the same thing happened. Melanie went to buy some cat food and the cashier said that she could not buy cat food, unless she proved that she had a cat. So she went home and brought her cat to the shop. Only after that was she allowed to buy the cat food. The next day Melanie went to the shop again. This time she brought a box with her. She went up to the same cashier and asked her to put her hand inside the box, so she did. The cashier said it felt warm and soft. Melanie then said "now that you're satisfied, please may I have some toilet paper."

*On her way home, Melanie came across this car dealership and she wanted a new car, so she decided to go in and get the information she needed.*

## 267. I want this color on my car or else

The next day Melanie was walking home from the supermarket. Her bag of groceries was especially heavy that day, and as she passed 'Hales used car dealership', she had an idea that she could drive herself to the supermarket and save a lot of time and aching muscles. She walked into the car dealership and as it just so happened, she got to speak to 'Hale' who was the owner himself. He asked her what kind of car she wanted and she replied "Well, sonny, I can't remember the name exactly, but it has something to do with hate or anger."
Hale replied "Well, let's see... Oh yes, you want a Plymouth Fury! We have a couple on the lot. What color do you prefer?"
Melanie has some trouble explaining the exact color to him, so she reached into her shopping bag, took out an ear of corn, stripped down the leaves and said "I want this color sonny."
To which Hale replied "Ma'am I'm sorry, but we don't have any in this color. Could I show you a nice blue one?"
"No son, I want this color."

"But ma'am, they didn't make that color! Maybe a cherry red one would suit you?" said the owner, obviously worried about losing a sale.

By this time, Melanie was angry and started throwing things at the owner, thereby chasing him out of the office and into the lot. One of the salesmen, coming into the office from the back door, noticed the disruption and asked the secretary what the old woman was so upset about.

The secretary replied "Apparently, Hale hath no Fury like

the woman's corn!"

*Some of Trump's children were now living on their own and wanted to send a gift to their mother for mother's day, but it seemed none of them knew their mother's taste very well.*

### 268. Why did you eat the parrot?

Three of Melanie and Trump's sons had left home; they went out on their own and prospered. Getting back together, they discussed the gifts they were able to give their elderly mother. The first said "I built a big house for our mother." The second said "I sent her a Mercedes with a driver." The third smiled and said "I've got you both beat. You remember how mom enjoyed reading the Bible? And you know she can't see very well. So I sent her a remarkable parrot that recites the entire Bible. It took elders in the church twelve years to teach him. He's one of a kind. Mom just has to name the chapter and verse, and the parrot recites it."

Soon thereafter, Melanie sent out her letters of thanks. She wrote to the first son "The house you built is so huge. I live in only one room, but I have to clean the whole house."

She wrote to the second son "I am too old to travel. I stay home most of the time, so I rarely use the Mercedes. And the driver is so rude!"

She wrote to her third son "You had the good sense to know what your mother likes, the chicken was delicious."

*Occasionally Trump and Melanie's grandchildren came to stay, but unfortunately Melanie never had the time to spend with them. One of the grandchildren wrote this poem dedicated to her.*

## 269. The internet is keeping Grandma busy

*In the dim and distant past*
*When life's tempo wasn't so fast,*
*Grandma used to rock and knit,*
*Crochet, tat and baby sit.*
*When the kids were in a jam,*
*They could always call on Gran.*
*But today she's in the gym*
*Exercising to keep slim*
*She's checking the web or surfing the net,*
*Sending some e-mail or placing a bet.*
*Nothing seems to stop or block her,*
*Now that Grandma's off her rocker.*

**Trump and Melanie were taking their grandchildren
back to their parents. They took the fast train so that
they could get them home before it got dark but it
seemed they got in the wrong train.**

## 270. The ticket is not for this train

An inspector was checking the tickets. When he got to Melanie
he said: "Sorry ma'am, this ticket is not for the very fast Train.
You can only use this ticket on the normal speed train."
She replied "well, then tell the conductor to drive slower"

**The kids were finally gone and old Melanie was
relaxing with her friends.**

## 270. I couldn't even reach that stroke

Melanie and her two elderly friends were sitting on a park bench
talking about old times when a flasher came by. The flasher
stood right in front of them and opened his trench coat.
Melanie had a stroke. Then the second old lady had a stroke. But

the third old lady . . . she couldn't reach that far.

**Melanie's memory problems were so severe, that she
could not even remember her best friend's name.**

## 271. How soon do you need to know my name?

Melanie and her best friend have known each other for many decades. Over the years they had shared all kinds of activities and adventures. Lately, their activities had been limited to meeting a few times a week to play cards.

One day they were playing cards when Melanie looked at her best friend and said "Now don't get angry with me, I know we've been friends for a long time, but I just can't think of your name! I've thought and thought, but I can't remember it. Please tell me what your name is."

Her friend glared at her. For at least three minutes, she just stared and glared at her. Finally she said "How soon do you need to know?"

*When Melanie was in her fifty's, she was looking at herself critically in the mirror and she was trying to get Trump to comfort her.*

## 272. Killer compliment

She pulled at the skin of her cheek, forehead, neck..., nothing eased her mind, and she could see each and every wrinkle. Desperately, she said to Trump "I look ugly and old with a lot of wrinkles. It's making me feel so depressed. What can you say that will cheer me up?" "You've got excellent eyesight." said Trump

*Trump was going away for a trip. He decided to play a joke on his wife but maybe he took it too far. He wrote her a letter which he left on the bed.*

## 273. I need some young blood

*Dear Melanie*

*You must realize that you are fifty four years old, and I have certain needs which you are no longer able to satisfy. I am otherwise happy with you as a wife, and I sincerely hope you will not be hurt or offended to learn that by the time you receive this letter, I will be at the Grand Hotel with my eighteen year old teaching assistant. I'll be home before midnight.*

*Your Husband Trump.*

When he arrived at the hotel, there was a faxed letter waiting for him that read as follows:

*Dear Trump,*

*You are seventy four years old, and by the time you receive this letter, I will be at the Breakwater Hotel with the eighteen year old pool boy. Since you are very good with numbers, you will appreciate that eighteen goes into fifty four more times than seventy four goes into eighteen. So don't wait up.*

*Your Wife Melanie*

**It is Trump and Melanie's thirtieth anniversary celebration and they decided to share some secrets with each other.**

## 274. How many times have you cheated on me?

Trump said to his wife "After so many years together, you can tell me how many men you cheated on me with?"

Melanie hesitated and said "Do you remember the loan for the house was refused to us and two days later, the bank called us to say it was approved?"

"Yes, so you only cheated on me once?"

"Well no, do you remember when you almost lost your job and a week later your boss told you that he was keeping you and you never worried about losing the job again?"

"So you cheated on me twice, and it was for good cause, so I forgive you... was that all?"

"Well no, do you remember when you wanted to run for office?" "Yes"

"Well you needed a thousand more signatures..."

**After many years Trump became very ill and fell into a coma.**

## 275. Why are you always around when something bad happens to me?

Trump had been slipping in and out of a coma for several months. Melanie had stayed by his bedside every single day. One day, when he came back from his coma, he motioned for her to come nearer. As she sat by him, he whispered, eyes full of tears "You know what? You have been with me all through the bad times. When I got fired,

You were there to support me. When my business failed, you were there. When I got shot, you were by my side. When we lost the house, you stayed right here. When my health started failing, you were still by my side. You know what?" "What dear?" she asked gently, smiling as her heart began to fill with warmth. "I think you're bad luck."

*All this stress over her husband's medical problems affected Melanie. She went to see her doctor, due to a case of chronic hiccups.*

## 276. Grandma you are pregnant

Melanie was at her doctor's office. She was being examined by one of the new doctors, but after about four minutes in the examination room, she burst out screaming and ran down the hall. An older doctor stopped her and asked what the problem was and she explained. He had her sit down and relax in another room. The older doctor marched back to the first and demanded "What's the matter with you? Melanie is sixty three years old, she has many grown children, many more young children and grand children and you told her she was pregnant?" The new doctor smiled smugly as he continued to write on his clipboard. "Cured her hiccups though, didn't it?"

*Trump recovered from his coma and immediately did something crazy. He spent a huge amount of money on a new car and got stopped by the police.*

## 277. I don't want her back

He was taking it for a test drive on the high way and was pushing it a bit. He had reached one hundred miles an hour; when he looked in his rear view mirror, he realized that a police car was following him, so again he accelerated. The police soon caught up with him and pulled him over. The police man got out and said "One hundred miles an hour!!! Are you mad or what!!!? I have half an hour before the end of my shift and I want to be lenient with you and let you go if you tell me the reason why you were driving at that speed and you better tell me something I have never heard before. Otherwise I will give you an enormous fine."

Trump thought for a while before he spoke "Long time ago, my wife ran away with a police man and I thought, shit, he is bringing her back! So I accelerated."

*The police man had to let him off the hook. Melanie has become too demanding with age and her children have decided it would be best if she went to a retirement home.*

### 278. Let me fart please

When she got there, she found that the staff were very attentive and took care of her well.

The nurses looked after her, washed her, served her delicious meals and seated her for meals so she could face the beautiful garden outside.

Everything seemed perfect. One day she was leaning her body to the right, the nurses quickly put her back straight again. Then she began leaning her body to the left, again the nurses quickly put her back straight.

A few days later, her family came to visit her.

"Is everything going well Grandma, do you like it here?"

"It's not bad at all, except they never let me fart."

*Now realizing that her favorite daughter didn't care much about her, Melanie changed her will.*

### 279. I want to be cremated

Melanie decided to prepare her Will and make her final requests. She told her Priest she had two final requests. Firstly, she wanted to be cremated and secondly, she wanted her ashes scattered all over Taj Casino. "Why Taj Casino?" asked the Priest. "Then I'll be sure my daughters will visit me twice a month."

*Trump was very sick and his children thought that this time around, this was the end.*

### 280. Is the funeral that soon?

Trump lay dying in his bed, while suffering the agonies of an impending death; he suddenly smelled the aroma of his favorite Italian Cookies wafting up the stairs. Gathering his remaining strength, he lifted himself from the bed. Leaning against the wall, he slowly made his way out of the bedroom and with even greater effort, gripping the railing with both hands, he crawled downstairs.

With labored breath, he leaned against the door frame, gazing into the kitchen; where if not for death's agony, he would have thought himself already in heaven, for there, spread out upon waxed paper, on the kitchen table, were literally hundreds of his favorite Cookies.

Was it heaven? Or was it one final act of heroic love from his children, seeing to it that he left this world a happy man? Mustering one great final effort, he threw himself towards the table, landing on his knees in a crumpled posture. His parched lips parted, the wondrous taste of the cookie was already in his mouth, seemingly bringing him back to life.

The aged and withered hand trembled on its way to a cookie at the edge of the table, when it was suddenly smacked with a spatula by Ivanka. "Back off!" she said, they're for the funeral."

*Trump did not die in that bed, although, he did have an unusual death. Melanie came back from the old age home to stay with Trump in his last hours*

## 281. The mule is going to jail

Melanie was tired of Trump's unmerciful nagging. From morning till night (and sometimes later), he was always complaining about something. The only time she got any relief was when she was out plowing with her old mule. She tried to plow a lot. One day, when she was out plowing, Trump brought her lunch in the field. She drove the old mule into the shade, sat down on a stump, and began to eat her lunch. Immediately, Trump began nagging her again. Complain, nag, complain and nag. It just went on and on. All of a sudden, the old mule lashed out with both hind feet, caught him smack in the back of the head and killed him dead on the spot. At the funeral several days later, the Minister noticed something rather odd. When a male mourner would approach Melanie, she would listen for a minute, then nod her head in agreement, but when a female mourner approached her, she would listen for a minute, then shake her head in disagreement. This was so consistent, the Minister decided to ask Melanie about it.

So after the funeral, the Minister spoke to Melanie and asked her why she nodded her head and agreed with the men, but always shook her head and disagreed with all the women. Melanie said "Well, the men would come up and say something about how nice my husband looked, or how he always dressed well so I'd nod my head in agreement." "What about the women?" The minister asked. "They wanted to know if the mule was for sale."

*Trump had passed away and Melanie went back to the old age home and grew more and more lonely.*

## 282. Eye for an eye

LearnFast Middle School had sponsored a luncheon for the elderly. At the luncheon Melanie had won a radio and was writing to say thank you.

*Dear LearnFast Middle School,*
*God bless you for the beautiful radio I won at your recent Senior Citizens Luncheon. I am Eighty four years old and live at the Safety Harbor Assisted Home for the Aged.*
*Most of my family members have passed away. I live alone now and it's nice to know that someone is thinking of me. God bless you for your kindness to an old, forgotten lady.*
*My roommate is ninety five and always had her own radio, but before I received one, she would never let me listen to hers, even when she was napping.*
*The other day her radio fell off the night stand and broke into a lot of pieces. It was awful and she was in tears.*
*She asked if she could listen to mine and I said fuck you.*
*Thank you for that opportunity.*
*Sincerely,*
 *Melanie"*

*Shortly after she wrote that letter, Melanie passed away and this was the day of her funeral.*

## 283. They were finally together

Melanie had many children with Trump. She had more children with different other men.

Standing before her coffin, the preacher prayed for her. He thanked the Lord for this very loving woman and said "Lord, they're finally together."

One mourner leaned over and quietly asked her friend "Do you think he means her first, second or third husband?" The friend replied "I think he means her legs."

*Melanie's two favorite children inherited her ranch and ...*

## 284. Heritage

Melanie's two favorite daughters inherited the family ranch. Unfortunately, after just a few years, they were in financial trouble. In order to keep the bank from repossessing the ranch, they needed to purchase a bull so that they could breed their own stock. The brunette balanced their check book and then took their last $600 dollars to another ranch where a man had a prize bull for sale.

Upon leaving, she told her sister "When I get there, if I decide to buy the bull, I'll contact you to drive out after me and haul it home." The sister arrived at the man's ranch, inspected the bull, and decided she wanted to buy it. The man told her that he could sell it for $599, no less. After paying him, she drove to the nearest town to send her sister a telegram to tell her the news.

She walked into the telegraph office, and said "I want to send a telegram to my sister telling her that I've bought a bull for our ranch. I need her to hitch the trailer to our pick-up truck and drive out here so we can haul it home." The telegraph operator explained that he'll be glad to help her and then added "It's just ninety nine cents a word."

After paying for the bull, the brunette only had $1 left. She realized that she'll only be able to send her sister one word. After thinking for few minutes, she nodded, and said "I want you to send her the word, 'comfortable'."

The telegraph operator shook his head. "How is she ever going to know that you want her to hitch the trailer to your pick-up truck and drive out here to haul that bull back to your ranch, if you send her the word 'comfortable'?"

The brunette explained "My sister's blonde, she'll read it slowly."

*Melanie died a short while after Trump and she was very happy to meet up with him again in the afterlife.*

### 285. Until death do you part?

"Ah, my Dear! I missed you so much, if only you knew how happy I am to finally be reunited with you here today."

Trump replied "Stop bugging me Melanie, the priest was clear when he said. "Until death do you part.!!""

# Chapter 11 x Conclusion

*Twitter's cousin was in an accident and Twitter had to go to the funeral. Here is how the accident happened.*

### 286. Who got me in this shit?

A bird was flying south for winter, but he had left too late and was frozen solid in a storm.

He dropped down into a pasture of cows. The biggest, fattest cow was doing a crap there, and the bird landed in it. At first he was disgusted, until he realized the poo was thawing him out!

He started crying out of joy as the ice melted. A cat that was nearby heard the cries, walked over, saw the bird and ate it

Morals to this story:

1. Not everyone who gets you into shit is your enemy
2. Not everyone who gets you out of shit is your friend
3. If you are in shit, keep your mouth shut

*Twitter had just left his cousin's funeral when he almost lost his life in another accident.*

### 287. The parrot is in jail

Before Trump passed away, he was driving speedily on his new Kawasaki at one hundred miles an hour on an empty road; all of a sudden he was face to face with a parrot which was struggling to fly. He did his best to avoid hitting the parrot, unfortunately it was too late and the collision was inevitable. He saw the parrot in his rear view mirror; the poor parrot was rolling over on the road and Trump felt sorry for it. He stopped his bike, came back to see the parrot lying on its back. He recognized the parrot 'Twitter' and picked it up and took it home with him and put it in a small cage with some food and water for when it woke up. The next day Twitter woke up, he saw the cage, the piece of bread and the water and he screamed out

"Shit! I have killed the biker and now I'm in jail."

*The next day Trump moved the parrot into a bigger cage. Because of the accident, Twitter had amnesia and the only word he could remember was YES.*

## 288. Yes...Yes...Yes

Trump's gas delivery had arrived but he was not home. He usually bought 20 gallons for the month. The gas delivery guy phoned him on his home phone to confirm the order and fill the gas containers. Twitter answered the phone.

"Hello, it's for the gas delivery, do I just deliver it as usual?" Twitter replied "Yes."

"We have a special price for two hundred gallons, do you want it?" "Yes."

"What about a full tank; its even cheaper per gallon, are you interested?"

"Yes"

When Trump returned home, he discovered a tank of gas in his garden. Trump immediately phoned his gas supplier. He argued with him for a while and finally realized what had happened. He took Twitter and nailed his wings to a cross to punish him.

"You will stay here for a month to teach you a lesson." The parrot saw another cross on the other side of the wall. "Hey, friend how long have you been there?" asked Twitter

The wooden made Jesus replied "Well, it's been almost two thousand years."

"Shit man!!! How many gallons of gas did you order?"

*Some say this is not how Twitter got himself on the cross and told the following story instead.*

## 289. Can I have nuts please?

Twitter went to a bar:

"Can I have nuts please?" he said.

"We don't sell nuts here" said the barman.

"Can I have nuts please?" repeated Twitter.

"I just told you, we don't sell nuts here."

"Can I have nuts please?"

"Listen little parrot if you repeat that to me once more, I will hang you there next to the Jesus."

"Can I have nuts please?" repeated Twitter

The barman hung the parrot next to Jesus on top of the cross.

The parrot turned toward Jesus and said "You also wanted nuts?"

**That was the story of Twitter the parrot, he is in some cross somewhere in the World.**

*What about our Chinese friend Fu? He went to Canada illegally. He applied for a refugee status and had to change his name.*

*Fu had just got to Canada with his wife illegally. His wife had just given birth and they both looked forward to seeing the baby. By the way their family name was 'Wong'.*

## 290. The Wongs gave birth to a white child

Mr. and Mrs. Wong got married and they had a child. They asked the nurse if they could see their child. The nurse brought their baby, but it was a white baby. The two of them said "But that's a white baby, and we are Chinese and two Wongs don't make a white."

*Not only was the boy white but it seemed that his name was also wrong.*

## 291. Sum ting Wong

What did the Chinese couple call their child?

Sum Ting Wong

*Now that his children were safely home, Fu concentrated on getting his refugee status in order and he went to the Canadian refugee department with his brothers.*

## 292. Why did they deport you?

Three Chinese brothers, Bu, Chu, and Fu, wanted to live legally in Canada. The brothers decided to change their names to sound more Canadian. Bu changed his name to Buck. Chu changes his name to Chuck and Fu got sent back to China.

*This book is a part of a series, be on the lookout for a condensed version of this book coming out in a picture format soon titled: LIFE OF A MAGA PRESIDENT.*
*Other Books being released soon:*
*-Meet Trump's Entourage*
*-Clintons after dark*

Follow the author on Twitter @nimus_y (NimusUnderscoreY) to get updates on new releases and also new exciting merchandise coming out soon